Millie's Wedding Dilemma

Contents

Dedication

To my two moms.
My mom, for helping give me ideas for this book and always
answering texts quickly, and my mother-in-law, a sweet
woman who is nothing like Mother Nola!

Chapter 1

1886 California

Millie stood on her tiptoes, reaching for a book for her father, Dr. William Hudson. Her fingers brushed against it as she made a frantic grab. Finally, it slipped just enough toward her to pull it free.

"Is this the one you wanted?" Millie asked, bringing over the heavy volume. It was dark red in color, but the lettering on the spine was so faded she couldn't make out what it said.

"Yes, that's it," her father agreed, pushing his glasses up his nose. "Thank you, my dear. I need it for my lecture tomorrow."

Millie's father was one of the finest professors at the local university. Not that she was biased. He'd been an incredible physician too, before the accident almost ten years prior that had taken her mother's life and left her father with two shattered legs and unable to be an attending doctor.

Though he was able to walk now with the aid of canes, and time had eased some of the pain at the loss of his wife and the profession he'd adored, he refused to give up his medical background and turned to giving lectures at the university and teaching classes. Something he could do with ease.

As much as she could, Millie helped him. They had an enormous library at home, and when her father wasn't teaching, he was reading.

"Might I bother you for one more?" her father asked. "The one I left over by the window."

"Of course," she answered. Handing him the book, she asked, "Shall I make us lunch?"

"That would be good," her father agreed, and then an expression crossed his face that made her worry.

"Papa! Are you feeling well?" she asked, hurrying over.

"Yes, my dear. I just...never mind. Yes, anything at all for lunch, please."

"No, you must tell me," Millie said, and sat close to him on the chair next to his desk. "I won't budge until you do." She crossed her arms to prove her point.

After a long sigh, her father nodded. "It's just I hate to see you like this."

"Like what?" Millie asked, confused.

He gestured with his hand. "Like this. Counting pennies. Spending your days helping this old man instead of enjoying your youth. Housework! Instead of choosing new dresses and having tea with friends, my daughter labors over chores. I feel I've let you down. We've gone from our large house with a housekeeper, a maid, and a cook to this cramped townhome." He put his head in his hands. "It pains me to see you suffer."

"Is that what's bothering you?" Millie asked. She leaned forward and kissed his cheek. "I'm quite happy, Papa. Why, this place is not so large I can't keep up with it. It's rather fun to make meals for you, and don't forget—we live in a lovely town with parks and gardens and many activities that do not cost. I enjoy myself tremendously. I do not suffer in the least."

"That is because you are a good girl," her father said, taking her hand. "But I cannot give you all you need. I know that." He was quiet for a moment. "Would you consider, perhaps, finding a young man? One to settle with, and perhaps make your life easier?"

Millie sat back in surprise. Honestly, the thought had never occurred to her. For as long as she could recall, she'd been happily looking after her father. If she left, who would help him?

"It would make this old man happy," he added.

"Papa, you aren't old," Millie scolded.

"But one day you will be, and I won't be here. I want my daughter to find happiness, and I want to be around to see it," he told her softly.

Millie didn't know what to say. Her father had never said such a thing, and it caused her to worry slightly. Was he unwell? Was that what prompted his concern? She replayed his words over again in her mind. No, he must be in good health since he said he wanted to be around to see her happy.

But...marriage? Millie gave him a small smile. "To be truthful, I've put no thought into it. But, if that's something you'd like me to do, I will. I am not committing to finding a husband, but if someone comes along that I like, I will consider it."

"Oh yes, that would make me happy, my dear. Just look around. That's all," he said.

She nodded and rose to make them lunch. The idea of her finding a man to marry was...slightly unsettling. Her concern was what would happen to her father. He couldn't manage by himself. She knew that. So why was he insisting? Was there some secret he wasn't telling her?

Millie sliced bread and put it on a plate on a tray. Going to the stove, she ladled out the pea soup, and added it to the tray. Just as she was about to carry it to her father, there was a knock on the kitchen door.

Crossing to the door quickly, Millie peered through the window, then opened it with a smile. "Hello, Jimmy," she said to the young boy before her.

"Letter for your father, Miss Millicent." He offered an envelope to her.

"Thank you," Millie answered. "Wait just a moment," she told him. "I haven't any pennies just now, but could I tip you with a cookie or two?"

"Yes, miss," the boy said eagerly.

She went into the kitchen and reached into the jar of freshly made oatmeal cookies and pulled out two. As soon as they were in Jimmy's hand, he'd run off.

Placing the letter on the lunch tray, Millie carried it to her father's study.

Though they called it his study, it was also the sitting room. Crammed with books covering most every surface and medical instruments of all kinds, Millie had grown up knowing the names and uses of almost each. They had come to her quickly, as she was around her father so often. At one point, she wanted to be a nurse, but taking care of her father was what was now needed.

Still, he assured her, she knew just as much, if not more, than most of the young women in nursing programs, so should she ever want to take up that pursuit, he knew she'd do well. The problem, however, was the fee to such a place. No longer with a large income, each coin that entered their household must be watched carefully. There was nothing to spare for such a dream.

"You've a letter," Millie said as she cleared away a handful of papers and set the tray on a side table.

"Oh? Bring it here, would you?" her father asked.

She nodded, and handed him the envelope, then busied herself with setting out his lunch while he read.

After a moment, her father said, "Millie, do you remember what we were talking about earlier?"

"About my perhaps finding a husband one day?" she asked lightly.

"Yes."

Millie stilled and looked at him in surprise. Her father was smiling. "I've received a letter from an old friend," he told her. "Her name is Rosemary. I didn't realize it, but she lives here in town."

"Oh?" Millie asked, unsure where he was going with this.

"Yes. She writes to tell me how sorry she was to have learned about your mother leaving us and the loss of my practice."

"That is kind of her," Millie replied, just a hint of questioning in her voice.

"She also mentions a gentleman," he went on. "A young doctor with an established practice here in town." He looked at her then, his brows slightly raised.

Millie crossed her arms. "Did you know about this doctor when you spoke with me a little bit ago?" she asked suspiciously.

"I didn't," her father promised. "However, she's invited us for tea, and him as well. Perhaps the two of you...might become acquainted? It doesn't hurt to at least meet him, since the opportunity has presented itself. If nothing else, we can enjoy a tea. I'd like to see how Rosemary has been all these years."

Millie bit her lip worriedly. While she had agreed to entertain the idea of a future with a husband, it had come just a little sooner than she'd imagined. Though her father was right, she could simply enjoy the tea and company, a small part of her wondered if more would come of it.

"What say you?" her father asked. "It's tomorrow afternoon."

"Tomorrow?" Millie felt a surge of panic. How could she be ready so quickly? Her eyes darted around the small house. There was so much to do. And what would she wear? Most of her clothes were terribly out of fashion.

Her father's eyes were fixed on her with a pleading look. She knew he never asked for much, and wouldn't ask this of her either. But it was obvious he was hoping that she would agree.

Millie sighed and threw her hands into the air. "Fine! But don't expect much to come of it."

"Of course," her father said, his face lighting up. "But if it does, then you have my blessing. He's a doctor, Millie. You know so much, you'd be an asset to him in his practice."

Millie laughed. "Papa, let's just see what happens! Who knows if he and I will even get along?"

But as Millie hurried to her room to find her least worn dress to prepare for tomorrow, a tiny little flutter formed in her stomach. What if they did get along? And what if something good came out of this?

Chapter 2

"Aunt Rosemary," Dr. Winston Felton asked as he sat at her table, "are you sure you think this young woman would be suitable? After all, neither of us have met her."

He was feeling apprehensive. The idea of marriage wasn't one he'd been entertaining, but his mother had made him feel quite guilty he'd not chosen a wife yet. At least, not one that she wanted. The woman his mother had wanted him to marry wasn't someone he could envision being with. Visiting Aunt Rosemary for her suggestions on young women had been a compromise.

"My dear nephew, I have never made a match that wasn't perfect. Why, think about your cousin Rose, and her husband, Levi."

"As I recall, they had already met—"

"No matter," his aunt replied in her throaty voice. "It was I who pushed them together. Lit the spark and made it happen." She waved her hand dramatically, striding across the room as though it were a stage. "You'll recall, she'd been sent to me to be married to a suitable man. I found one."

Winston nodded, deciding not to argue with her. Aunt Rosemary was nothing if not sure of herself. She shared that trait with her sister, his mother.

Never mind the rest of the story was that Aunt Rosemary was quite scandalized at the time of Rose and Levi's meeting. He smiled to himself. That all said, it was true. She had matched several people and things had worked well for them.

Perhaps she could do the same for him. It would make his mother happy, make Aunt Rosemary happy, and hopefully, the most important of all, make him and his wife happy. If he was to marry, it would be for love and nothing less.

Aunt Rosemary picked up a small book and flipped through it. Winston tried not to stare. He'd heard of Aunt Rosemary's book before, but he'd never seen it.

Her book, or more likely by this point, books, were filled with information about everyone she knew and even those she didn't. Every detail was included. It was a habit his mother said had been started in her girlhood.

"Found it. Are you listening?" Aunt Rosemary asked. At his nod, she read, "Millicent Hudson. Age twenty-four, daughter to a doctor. Mother was a school teacher. Parents were in a carriage accident about ten years ago." Aunt Rosemary looked up at him then, her voice lowering. "This is the information I recently received. Her mother passed. Her father, once a very talented doctor, had his legs severely injured. As a result, he no longer can practice, and instead teaches at the local university."

"Why can't he practice?" Winston asked.

His aunt looked at him with a frown. "He can't walk well. A doctor must make his rounds."

"Perhaps," Winston said, "but there is much that can be done at the bedside or to treat in a clinic."

She shrugged. "I wouldn't know, dear boy, that's your department. Now, they'll be coming for tea. There's something else you must know."

"And that is?"

"Her family no longer has money, after the accident."

"That doesn't bother me," Winston said.

No, money, reputation, and class were things more important to his mother. His father, a wealthy landowner and businessman, had never cared much either. A tool, he'd called money. Nothing more.

"I've enough, and then some." Winston stood and paced for a moment. "What I'm wanting, though, is someone I can love. Someone I can get along with. Who makes me feel happy to be around. I'd also like someone who would be capable of helping me in my practice a few mornings a week."

"Which is why she'd be perfect, I'm sure," Aunt Rosemary said. "Your mother will be quite upset that the girl doesn't have means. However, that has become difficult to find as of late, with you young people caring less and less about your position in society." She shuddered, no doubt thinking of his cousin Rose.

"Perhaps Mother will be upset," Winston said slowly. "But I'm still not sure I am ready to settle. I could have all of those things I want without a wife."

"Your mother says otherwise," his aunt said, pouring herself a cup of tea. "And your mother—and I—know best. She was quite upset you didn't marry Ceclia."

"So was Ceclia," Winston snorted. "But it wasn't me she loved. It was my reputation and money. I'm far happier without her."

Aunt Rosemary opened her mouth to answer when there was a knock at the parlor door. "That must be them now." She squinted at him critically. "Don't slouch. Straighten your jacket. Remember, you are not just representing yourself, but your entire family."

Winston grimaced, but did as she ordered. With Aunt Rosemary, it was easier that way.

She nodded, a pleased expression on her face, then crossed the room to the parlor door, opened it, and smiled. "Dr. Douglas Husdon. You are a sight for sore eyes." She embraced the man who stood before her. They blocked the doorway so Winston couldn't see the young woman who was there as well, only a bit of her skirt.

"Ah, Rosemary! It's been so long. How have you been? Has life treated you well?"

"Better than you," she said, raising a brow.

The doctor laughed. "It's true, but I'm content. I enjoy teaching and my daughter is my joy." He slowly hobbled further into the room, a cane in each hand. "Hello," he said warmly, managing to balance and offering a hand when he spotted Winston.

Winston stepped forward and took the outstretched palm. He returned the firm handshake and met the other doctor's eyes. They were friendly, kind. Without even knowing anything about him, Winston instantly knew he liked him.

"And this must be Millicent," Aunt Rosemary said, her gaze sweeping over the young woman.

"Millie, if you don't mind," the young woman said. She moved into the room and Winston felt his breath catch.

There, before him, was a small woman with light brown hair, a perfectly shaped face, and wide eyes that were just as kind as her father's. Her voice was sweet and pleasing to his ears. Could it be his aunt Rosemary had, in fact, found a woman who interested him?

Winston tried not to stare at Millie. But already, he liked what he saw. His mother would have pointed out her dress was older, not the latest style or some such, but he wouldn't have been able to tell. All he knew was that she radiated goodness. And he liked that.

"Let's have tea," Aunt Rosemary said, settling herself at the table.

Millie pulled out a chair for her father and sat next to him. Winston took the chair opposite of hers. When he looked at her, she met his eyes and blushed, then looked down.

Her father spoke then, a welcome relief to him, and Millie, based on her expression. "So tell me, Dr. Fulton, what kind of patients do you treat?"

"Winston, please," he answered. "I'm a generalist. I've a large home here in town and have an office attached with a waiting room, supply room, and a treatment room."

Millie's father nodded. "I used to do the same, with an identical setup, years before back in Oregon. That's where I met your aunt some years ago. She was one of my patients once, when she was visiting her niece."

"And you did a fine job of helping me," Aunt Rosemary nodded. "I'll always be grateful to you." She leaned forward and whispered, "I got a terrible rash from some native plant!" She shuddered.

"What made you move here?" Winston asked, offering the plate of small sandwiches to the doctor and Millie.

As they each took a few, her father sighed, "When my wife passed away, after my injuries healed, I hoped for a fresh start. The university here offered me a position. I took it. There's not much more a man such as me can do."

"I disagree," Winston said. He noticed Millie stare at him.

"Do you?" she asked, softly.

If he wasn't mistaken, there was a flicker of hope in her eyes. "Yes," Winston said. "Would you ever be interested in treating patients again?"

Millie's father swallowed hard, and a tortured look came over him. "It's all I want," he said quietly.

"Then, if I might be so bold to make a suggestion?" Winston asked.

He really had no idea why he was about to say what he was. Was it the hopeful look in Millie's eyes? The pang of knowing what it would feel like to have this career, something he was incredibly passionate about, yanked away without any way to continue to live his dream of helping others?

Dr. Hudson was looking at him, a puzzled look on his face. Millie looked much the same. "I could use someone one day a week for my in-clinic patients," he said, "while I make rounds to those too elderly or injured to visit me. Would you be willing?"

With a gasp, Millie turned to her father, tears springing to her eyes. Her father looked shocked, one of the tiny sandwiches halfway to his mouth. "But...I cannot walk well," he said.

"We will adjust the schedule so that the only patients that day are those you can see while sitting. You don't need to walk to take a pulse, check someone's wrist or ankle, or check a red throat." Winston smiled. "You'd be doing me a favor, really, if you'd consider it. I'll have transportation waiting for you each time, before and after, if you'll consider doing this."

"Papa," Millie gasped. She reached over and squeezed his hand. Then she smiled at Winston. He could have sworn it lit up the room. One thing he was sure of, was there would never be anything as wonderful as her smile.

"If you... are sure?" Dr. Hudson said, hesitantly.

"Quite sure," Winston said confidently. "Just as sure as I know, Miss Hudson, I'd love it if you'd accompany me on a walk after our tea?"

The smile she gave him was so genuine, so stunningly breathtaking, Winston felt as though his heart would burst. It was fortunate there was another doctor on hand, just in case that happened. He knew, without any hesitation, that Millie was someone he wanted to spend more time with.

Perhaps even marry.

Chapter 3

Millie glanced shyly at Winston. She could hardly believe the last three weeks. First, by an absolute miracle, Dr. Fulton had restored the happiness and joy to her father that had been deeply missing, by asking him to do clinic hours for him one day a week.

He had even made it sound as though it was to be a favor for him. Had he really done it just to be kind to a fellow doctor? Or was it because he was trying to win her hand? Millie wasn't sure. At the moment, she also didn't care. He was incredibly thoughtful, and that alone was enough to make her look fondly at him.

Her father hadn't been so happy in years. Each Monday morning, the day he didn't have classes at the university until the late afternoon, he donned his best suit and waited eagerly for the gig to arrive to pick him up. Each time,

Winston had picked him up, and a hired wagon took her father to the university afterward.

"How about a lemonade?" Winston asked as they neared a seller in the park.

"That would be lovely," Millie agreed, and they paused by a man in a striped suit selling bottles of the cool, sweet and tart drink.

Winston held the bottles in his hand and walked over to a bench. A yellow and black butterfly fluttered and landed on Millie's arm before flying away again. He smiled as she laughed in delight.

"Thank you for joining me," he told her, offering one of the bottles. "I enjoy our walks together."

"So do I," Millie said. They sat in a comfortable silence for a moment, the only sound the birds and the rustling of leaves, then she said, "I can't thank you enough for all you've done for Papa. He's like a new man."

"I have done nothing but help a fellow human," Winston told her. "Though the fact it brings you a measure of happiness is a reward that I am happy to claim."

Her cheeks colored. "You flatter me."

"Not at all," Winston said. "You know we are both the same. Practical minded. We've learned that. I speak from practicality on the matter. It brings me joy to see your happiness."

He turned to her then. "Millie, I know we've not known each other long, but I think we are well suited for each other. Would you consider marrying me? Perhaps it's too soon for love in your heart, but I promise you, since I met you, I've done nothing but think about you every waking moment of the day."

Her breath caught. Winston was correct. They were both similar and also thought in a logical way. It was part of why she liked him. He also wasn't false. There had been no flattering that didn't feel genuine. He never boasted, which was a surprise. Somehow, she had expected that. It was wonderful she'd been proven wrong.

Winston was an incredible person. Everything he did was with one intent, and that purpose being to help others. Outside of her father, Millie had never met anyone who was so concerned with helping others. It made her proud to know him.

And, if she was to be quite truthful, she was attracted to him. Winston was a good deal older than her, nearing thirty-five, but that didn't matter to her at all. She liked that he was mature, settled, knew what he wanted in life, and wasn't flighty.

The question was, however, what did she feel about marriage? Her heart knew that she felt something for him, something that would likely develop into a lasting love. She longed to say yes. But...what of her father?

Millie felt tortured. She knew she must speak though, or else he might mistake her anguish for lack of interest.

But, as soon as she opened her mouth, Winston said, "Are you worried about your father?"

She nodded. "Yes. How will Papa get along without someone to help him and cook meals for him?"

Winston took another sip of his drink. "I think a housekeeper is what he needs," he said finally. "I feel sure Aunt Rosemary can find one of impeccable respectability. Her wages will be my responsibility, as a thanks to him for helping me."

"Oh!" Millie gasped. "That is too wonderful. Papa would never agree."

"Then we must make him," Winston said, standing. He took her hand, turned her palm up, and pressed a kiss to her wrist. "I hope to marry you soon."

A shiver went through Millie and she smiled up at him. "Then, yes. Yes, I'd love to marry you, Winston."

He pulled her up into his arms, gave a soft kiss to her lips, and gazed lovingly at her. "You make me the happiest man alive, Millie. I know we will be incredibly happy together."

Millie knew it as well.

The next few weeks were an absolute whirlwind. A housekeeper came, found by Aunt Rosemary, and Millie took to her instantly. Her father agreed to let Winston pay for her wages, but only under the condition he be allowed to help work off the debt. As a result, Winston allowed him to work an afternoon with him once a week as well.

If Millie had thought her father happy before, he was ecstatic.

Two days before the wedding, Winston came to their small house. He wore a concerned look on his face.

"Whatever is wrong?" Millie asked, taking his hands in hers. The distress on his face wasn't something she'd ever seen before, and it alarmed her.

Winston squeezed her hands and led her to a small sofa. He was quiet for so long it made her nervous. Finally, he said, "You know my mother is a widow?"

"I do," Millie answered.

"Well, she has decided to move here. To town."

"That's wonderful," Millie said, sitting back. "I'm sure I shall enjoy her company very much."

Winston cringed, and Millie wondered at his odd expression.

"Perhaps," he said slowly. "I've no doubt you will try. My mother, not so much. You know I have told you she is critical, opinionated to the point of rudeness, and also very shallow." He took a deep breath. "My dear, I have some news, and I do hope that you won't change your mind about becoming my wife."

Millie laughed then. "My love, there is nothing you could tell me to convince me not to marry you."

But Winston's expression wasn't one of surety. He squeezed her hands again and said, "My mother has decided she will be moving in with us."

Chapter 4

Winston straightened his jacket and hurried into his office. In truth, he was glad for the escape from the house, as he was sure his bride of only three weeks also was.

From the day his mother had moved in, just four days after he and Millie had said "I do" everything had turned upside down.

No, that wasn't quite accurate.

It was as if life was turned upside down, shaken all about, thrown into a box, shaken some more, and then upended upon the floor for them to stare in shock at the disarray. Yes, that was more accurate.

The first moment she'd walked into the house and Winston had introduced her to Millie, the problems had begun.

"It is so good to have you here, Mother Nola," Millie had said with her usual sweet smile. She reached a hand out, but his mother had pushed right past her.

"Ah, did you have a good journey here?" Millie tried again.

When his mother didn't answer, she turned to Winston with a confused look.

After his mother had slowly turned around the foyer she crossed her arms. "So you are the one responsible for this disaster?" his mother sniffed loudly.

Millie glanced around, trying to see just what she was talking about, what could possibly be considered a disaster, but his mother had walked into the kitchen, and they trailed behind her. "No coffee made? No tea? You are neglecting my son!"

Millie stared in shock at Winston, who put his arm around her. "I'm sure—"

"Winston!" his mother barked, standing before them again. "Why don't you see to your mother's bags? She has to lug them up the stairs herself? Tsk! Has she even gotten my room ready?"

Millie stood, trying not to tremble under the fierce gaze of her mother-in-law, who was squinting at her. He moved closer, wanting to protect her. "Your room is ready, Mother. Millie and the housekeeper saw to it, and I'll carry your bags up shortly."

"Pretty enough," his mother finally said, and she finished her appraisal of Millie, but then sniffed again. "I liked Ceclia better though. She was a woman with class."

Through gritted teeth, Millie answered, a fixed smile on her face, "I am delighted to have you here, Mother Nola. I look forward to spending time with you."

Winston tensed as his mother remarked, "You would. You are a low-class girl. Of course, you would think to be elevated by me."

While Millie stood there sputtering, Winston frowned. "Mother, what a terrible thing to say. Remember, this is my home, and Millie is my chosen wife. I'll not have you treat her this way."

Millie leaned into Winston's strong arm that was wrapped around her shoulder.

"It's the truth though, isn't it?" his mother had asked. "She's a girl from a poor family? That's what Rosemary said. Your aunt has an impeccable eye."

Winston winced as the words flooded his mind. He knew his mother had hurt Millie, but Millie continued to be kind. Really, he didn't deserve her.

Hurriedly, Millie followed him into his office. He glanced her way lovingly. Millie made him so happy. He just hoped he did the same for her.

In her starched dress and white apron covering it, Millie sat at a small desk with a look of such relief for having escaped his mother's newest tirade over the lack of fresh flowers in the sitting room that he felt terrible guilt. And that he must apologize.

Again.

"Millie," he began.

She looked up and smiled at him. "All is well," she said, though her expression didn't quite speak the truth.

"My mother," he started.

"Is a trying individual," Millie sighed. "But I am also trying. Trying to do my best. And we will come to an understanding at some point, I am sure," she said. "Her dislike for me can't last forever. Perhaps one day something I do shall please her."

"I appreciate that," Winston said, and leaned over to kiss her before his patients arrived. He hoped she was right. His mother was excellent at holding grudges. That was why she'd refused to come to his simple wedding, when he'd refused a lavish affair for her to be in charge of. And the bride she'd wanted in place of Millie.

"As I appreciate everything you do," Millie said. She shrugged. "I can't help not being just what she wanted, but I am doing my hardest to get along with her."

"I know," Winston said gloomily, and ran a hand over his dark brown hair. "Mother doesn't make it easy."

"That's an understatement," Millie muttered. He thought it best not to reply.

No matter that Aunt Rosemary had liked Millie, his mother would hear nothing that would contradict her opinions. While his mother was usually polite to Millie in front of him, he had no doubt in his mind that she was unkind in what she said when he wasn't there. Why was she that way?

And why had she wanted to move in with him, here in the crowded city she didn't like? Usually she traveled, as she had since his father passed away. For her to be in one place for so long was strange.

He really had no idea why she was there, but he could tell it was making Millie unhappy, and that made his heart ache. Though they hadn't been married for long, Winston couldn't imagine life without her. She meant the world to him, and his days would be empty without her smile, or touch, or presence.

Even now, though they were simply working, he felt at peace, knowing she was there. Winston looked over, and Millie smiled at him. "It's going to be a busy morning," she warned. "You've eight patients on the schedule."

"It could be worse," Winston said. He walked over and read over her shoulder. "Hmm. Nothing too serious it seems." He peered through the window. "Ah, here comes someone now. Luckily, I have just enough time to do this." Leaning down quickly, he kissed Millie once more, leaving her red-cheeked and with a giggle as the door opened and Mr. Baker walked in.

"Mr. Baker," Winston greeted. "Let's go look at that knee of yours, shall we?"

The door between the house and the office creaked open, and Winston saw his mother come through. As he ushered the patient into the examination room, he frowned. He'd told her—begged her—not to use that door as it wasn't professional.

Millie jumped to her feet. Winston was grateful for her. He just hoped that his mother didn't chase her away. He'd raised that concern last night, when they were reading in bed. Millie had laughed, but then teased, asking him if that was indeed an option.

As the door closed behind him and Mr. Baker started to talk about his knee, Winston hoped desperately he'd not put an idea into Millie's head. With the way his mother was acting, he wouldn't blame her one bit.

Chapter 5

Millie took a deep breath and released it slowly. She'd read in a medical book that slow, deep breathing was good for stress. That was something she had a great deal of right now. Far more than she'd like.

From the first moment Mother Nola had arrived, each interaction with her had been quite unpleasant. There were times her mother-in-law was less ghastly than others, but the majority of the time, Millie couldn't wait to escape each morning to help run the front room of Winston's office.

It also gave her a chance to spend time with her father. He was still as happy as ever to see patients there, and several, much to his delight, had requested him specifically.

Millie enjoyed the patients herself. It was always nice to talk with them for a few moments or help bring some small comfort to those suffering, with a cup of tea or a peppermint that Winston kept at the ready for just such a moment. Occasionally, he or her father asked her to help in the capacity of nurse, and she eagerly did.

If only every day was like the mornings. Well, most of the mornings. Sometimes, there was an unwelcome event.

Creeeeek.

The door between the office and house pushed open slowly. Winston glanced over. His mother's head was sticking through.

Millie gave him a reassuring smile, and stood. Though she'd rather do anything but see what Mother Nola needed, Winston couldn't be disturbed when he was attending to patients. Mother Nola knew that, which was why she was motioning to Millie.

Being an unwelcome event.

Mother Nola also knew that Winston didn't like her using that door to interrupt unless it was an emergency. Which, this most obviously was not. In fact, none of her interruptions had been.

With a last deep breath, and a smile she hoped didn't look forced, Millie went into the house and quickly shut the office door behind her. "Did you need me, Mother Nola?"

"I was bored. The housekeeper is out. I want someone to make me tea."

Millie closed her eyes for just a moment, then turned to the kitchen. There was no use arguing. It would only delay things and she was needed back in the office to help keep everything running smoothly. She bustled about, hurriedly filling the kettle and setting the water to boil. Winston's mother watched her every move.

A mixture of irritation, guilt, and frustration filled Millie. Irritation at her mother-in-law acting as though Millie were hers, to wait on her hand and foot. Guilt, because she shouldn't feel this way. It was obviously also a trying event for Winston's mother, and she should practice harder at being kind and patient.

Then there was the frustration. A lot of frustration. There were many times she simply wanted to scream or growl or shake Mother Nola. And that's when the guilt returned. So, Millie simply smiled, even if she didn't always feel as though she wanted to, and did her best. That was all she could do.

"Do you need anything else before I go back and arrange the patient files?" Millie asked once the water had heated sufficiently. It wasn't true what they said. A watched kettle did boil. Watching it was the best way for her temper not to boil over.

"Something to eat," her mother-in-law said. She sniffed. "You surely don't expect me to have tea without an accompaniment? I'm not a peasant."

Millie counted again slowly. Her jaw ached from clenching it. "The housekeeper made some lovely cookies yesterday," Millie finally answered, and set a few on a plate. "Spice cookies, as I recall."

She set them on the table next to the tea. Mother Nola just stared at her. "If...if there's nothing else, I'll go," she said. Her mother-in-law's expression unsettled her, and she was anxious to leave and return to a friendlier atmosphere. That was another thing she sometimes felt. Unsettled. It was difficult never knowing what to expect with her mother-in-law. The woman was very good at keeping her on her toes.

Millie had almost made it back to the office door when her mother-in-law, following behind her, said in a critical tone, "I don't know what Winston sees in you, other than you are a hard worker."

Her heart thudding, Millie stilled. She didn't turn back around. Quite honestly, she wasn't sure what to do. The critical comments her mother-in-law said were never made when Winston was around, though she knew he suspected they were said. She supposed that she should be happier this time that there was a compliment mixed in.

Millie didn't wish to complain, but her heart ached each time her mother-in-law spewed venom. She also wondered how long she could manage to hold her tongue. It was getting much harder. The occasional kind thing said wasn't enough to erase the sting or hurt that felt constant.

She tried to be kind, to be respectful and do all her mother-in-law asked, but the woman just made it so difficult.

Millie took in a slow, deep breath. She held it, counting to ten, then slowly released it.

"You are just fine around his office, but a woman of good standing in the town, that you won't ever be. Not even as a distinguished doctor's wife. You don't have the looks for it. Ceclia, ah, she is an angel. Beautiful. Floated on air. From a good family. She came from good stock, and it showed. I'll never understand why Winston didn't marry her."

Her chest was tight now, and Millie found it hard to breathe. As she reached for the doorknob, her hand trembled. She debated saying something, but didn't, and slid back into the office, this time making sure the door was locked from the office side.

Millie sat at her desk, her throat thick with tears. It was an unusually slow day. The office appeared empty. Winston must have left to do his rounds, for her father called from the examination room, "Is that you, Millie?"

"Yes, Papa," she said. "Did you need me?"

There was a shuffling sound, and her father walked out, using his canes to support himself. He sat in one of the patient chairs. "No, my dear, but I think you need me."

The tears she hadn't wanted to release sprang out then. "Oh, Papa! She's horrible! I can't stand being so nice to her." She buried her head into her father's shoulder. "She's just so unkind to me."

"It's because she loves Winston, and she's afraid to share his love with someone else," her father said, stroking her head.

"What she doesn't realize is Winston has room in his heart for both of you, and for children too when they come. Perhaps..." he was quiet a moment, "perhaps she is also extra miserable right now, because she's alone. Remember, she lost her husband. I can tell you from experience that the ache and emptiness never fades away completely, but it is worse in the first few years."

Millie sat up and wiped her eyes. "You are right, Papa. I'm trying. And I'll simply try harder. After all, Mother Nola will be in my life for a long time. I'd much rather be friends with her, then not."

"That's my girl," her father said, and the pride in his voice warmed her.

Though she might not have any affection from her mother-in-law, Millie knew she had her father's, and Winston's. That made her feel comforted.

The door to the office opened, and Millie returned to her desk, while her father greeted his patient, and they moved into the examination room.

Yes, her father was right. Perhaps if she saw things from Mother Nola's point of view, she could be more loving and kind and forgiving of the hurtful things she said.

Perhaps.

The morning passed, and Millie was relieved to see Winston return. Her father left for the university, and Winston pulled over a chair next to her.

"I've missed you," he said.

"I've missed you too," Millie answered.

Winston searched her face for a long moment. "She was unkind again, wasn't she?"

"It's nothing I can't handle," Millie promised him. "I think..." and her father's words returned to her, "I think that she's just having trouble accepting that you have room in your heart for both of us."

Taking her hand gently in his, Winston kissed her palm. "You are an incredible woman, and I couldn't ask for a better wife. I do have some news, though, and I hope it won't be upsetting for you."

"Why would it be?" Millie asked.

"I have been invited to a medical conference in a few days. When I spoke to the people hosting, I mentioned I'd like your father to attend as well. They agreed."

"That's wonderful," Millie gasped. "Papa will be delighted!"

"Yes, I think so. But there are two problems." Winston gave her a concerned look. "First, I will have to leave you for a week. Second, that means you'll be here alone with Mother."

"Ah." Millie was silent for a moment.

She was sure if she asked Winston not to leave that he would stay, however, how could she do that to him? And how could she do that to her father, who was enjoying himself, back in a practice for the first time in years?

"Well," Millie finally answered, "we won't quite be alone. The housekeeper will be here. I'm sure that both your mother and I will find plenty to do to keep ourselves occupied. You need not worry about us."

Winston searched her face once more. "You are sure?" he asked.

"Yes. I will miss you terribly, but I am sure this must be important for you to attend, and Papa will enjoy himself tremendously. You are so incredibly sweet to take him."

"He is a talented physician," Winston told her. "But beyond that, I know it brings you happiness to see him doing what he loves, and I would do anything to bring you joy."

"Then return safe to me," Millie said with a smile, as she moved closer to him.

Winston's arms pulled her close, just as *creeeeeeeaaak*. The door between the office and the house opened.

"Winston," Mother Nola said. "I simply must talk with you. About...your wife."

Chapter 6

Winston leaned against the plush seat on the train. He'd paid for first-class tickets for himself and Millie's father. Her father was completely absorbed in a thick medical book he'd brought. The man never stopped expanding his knowledge. It made Winston smile. He wanted to be that way himself, but today, though he held a newspaper in his lap and tried to read, he couldn't stay focused.

Worry about Millie filled his mind. It wasn't because he doubted Millie's ability to care for herself while he was gone. No, it was because he felt incredibly guilty at leaving her alone with his mother. But he also had guilt at each instance he felt irritated with his mother.

Like when she'd interrupted them in his office, saying she wanted to speak with him about Millie. Millie had pretended not to hear and had gone to straighten up the back room of the clinic. As his mother had pulled him into the house, to show the travesty of her favorite brand of tea sitting empty, and her insistence that Millie must have used it all, and without her permission, Winston had sighed.

"Mother, Millie did not drink your tea. The housekeeper told you there was none at the store, but she had specially ordered an entire case of it, and it would arrive this week. That was as she made you the last of it yesterday evening. Don't you remember?" He had tried not to push a hand through his hair or sigh in frustration, but he was quite irritated.

Once again, he'd told his mother to stop blaming Millie for everything she didn't like. As usual, his mother had acted hurt, and accused him of not taking her concerns seriously. Then she left the room. A short time later, he'd seen her leaving the house.

Concern over what might be happening back home, even at this very moment, filled him. Winston raised the paper and tried again to read. It was of no use. He wouldn't feel better until he was back home.

He focused his gaze outside the window, watching trees and the occasional building blur past. It would have been hypnotic, lulled him to sleep, had he not been so worried about what was happening with Millie and his mother.

The train ride took most of the day, and when they arrived at the station, Winston hailed transportation to take him and Dr. Hudson to the hotel where they were staying. He also sent a note to Millie, letting her know where he was in case of an emergency.

The next several days passed slowly. Winston hardly slept, even though he was exhausted by the end of the day. In the evenings, with nothing to occupy his mind, his thoughts turned to Millie and his worry about what might be happening without him to act as a sort of shield for her.

He also couldn't shake this feeling that something was happening. He just didn't know what. The sooner they returned, the better, and he looked forward to the return trip. He just hoped that his mind was playing tricks on him, and there wasn't a reason to be as concerned as he was.

Chapter 7

Millie luxuriated in the fact it was nearly lunchtime and not once had Mother Nola screeched her name. This was the fourth day in a row she'd hardly seen her mother-in-law. It was quite relaxing, honestly. And a welcome relief, as once Winston had left for the train, his mother had insulted Millie, telling her how she should be more grateful that Winston made a point to include her crippled father in his business and help her rise from poverty.

It had taken all Millie had within her not to lash out. Winston's mother could be as cruel as she liked to her, but she wouldn't tolerate any insults about her father. The look on her face must have made that clear, because she'd not gone near Millie since.

Still, her words swirled around in Millie's head, echoing and never leaving her. Was her mother-in-law trying to get rid of her or force her to leave? She found excuses quite often to bring up Ceclia, just to see how Millie would react. Usually, Millie would just smile and nod, or ignore it if she could, but each time was a little dig into her.

Winston had assured her, and Millie believed him, that his heart was hers. Both of them had felt that instant connection, of that she had no doubt. It truly felt like love at first sight. She also knew he hadn't cared for Ceclia. But it still pricked her, knowing that she wasn't as pretty, as petite, as accomplished, as rich.

She'd admitted as much to Winston, and he'd provided his own list. His made her smile. Smarts, Winston said. That was one thing she had plenty of that Ceclia didn't have. Also patience, kindness, and many other virtues that were far more important to him.

The thought made her miss him, and she hoped he and her father were doing well. She couldn't wait until they returned home.

The front door opened, and Millie frowned. Had someone come in? She called out, "Hello?"

There was no answer. Hadn't she been alone? Maybe it was the housekeeper. Or Mother Nola? Millie moved to the window. She didn't see anyone leaving the house. However, across the street, a man in a slightly older jacket and a cap covering most of his face stood facing their home.

Millie stood behind the curtain, pulling it back just enough to watch. He seemed to be waiting. For what? And who was he?

Prickles crawled up her spine. Millie desperately hoped he wasn't keeping an eye on the house to rob it. She also hoped that she was incorrect and she wasn't home alone.

She went into the kitchen, but the housekeeper wasn't there. Millie visited each room of the house, but she was alone. The fact made her feel nervous. Going into the parlor, which had windows facing the same direction as when she'd first spotted the man, Millie peered out again. He was gone.

It must have just been a coincidence.

Relief flooded her. She'd be so grateful when Winston returned. Her imagination was playing tricks on her.

Millie spent the afternoon reading. Well, she tried to anyway. Her eyes would drift constantly to the window, to the spot across the street where she'd seen the man.

A few hours later, the front door opened and then closed. Millie set her book down and rose, nearly running into her mother-in-law.

"Forgive me," Millie said.

Mother Nola sniffed, giving her usual expression of dissatisfaction. "Where's the housekeeper? I don't smell dinner."

"I'm not sure," Millie said. "I am sure she will be back soon. It's her market day."

Mother Nola turned to go up the stairs. Millie hesitated, then asked, "By chance, have you noticed a man lingering about?"

Her mother-in-law froze. Millie immediately regretted what she'd said. She'd frightened the woman, likely, based on the way she'd stiffened. Mother Nola turned, and Millie knew she was right. There was a look on her face that was one of worry. Mother Nola didn't care for the overcrowding of the city, often fretting over the crime and crowds. Now, she'd gone and given her another reason to dislike it.

"A man, lurking?" she asked, with a faint tremble. "What...what did he look like?"

"I'd never seen him before," Millie said. "He was across the street, seeming to watch the house. He wore an older coat and a cap pulled down low over his face."

"Perhaps he was one of Winston's patients," Mother Nola said, though she didn't sound convinced. Then she sniffed, and took on a haughty tone. "He makes himself available to anyone. Even those of the lower class. But you knew that already, didn't you?"

Millie stiffened. She opened her mouth to say something, but her mother-in-law was already going up the steps. So, she closed her eyes a moment, and turned to the kitchen at the sound of someone in it.

The housekeeper was back, and starting the evening meal. Millie was relieved not to be alone any longer. Even if that meant she had her mother-in-law's insults.

No. Why should she always accept them? Wasn't she due respect, as a human, as Winston's wife, and as a good person? She was.

Millie closed her eyes. Anger filled her. She didn't know how long she stood there, practicing in her mind what she knew she ought to say, but some time had passed. Footsteps sounded on the stairs, and Mother Nola came into the foyer. Millie opened her mouth before she realized she'd spoken.

"You need to apologize."

"Apologize?" Mother Nola raised her eyebrows. "For what? For raising a son as compassionate as he is, that he'd take in a penniless half-orphan?"

Millie sucked in a breath. Her voice wobbled and tears sprang to her eyes. "No. For being a venomous old woman who has nothing kind to say and is cruel. Since the day you came, you've treated me horribly. You say unkind things about me. I understand you don't like me. But I've tried, and you've no right to treat me this way, not when I've done nothing but been kind."

Mother Nola opened her mouth, but Millie pressed on. "We used to have money. We used to live in a home much nicer than this one. But one day, my parents were returning late from a party. It was dark and raining. When going around a curve, the carriage slid and swung too close to a bank."

Though her throat was tight, Millie continued. She angrily wiped the tears from her cheeks. "It tumbled down the bank. Father pulled my mother from the carriage. He returned to help the others who were inside. My mother joined him, trying to rescue the horses that were screaming in terror.

"The driver was trapped under the carriage. Just as my father got him free, my mother released one of the panicked horses. It kicked, knocking her down. As it ran, it threw Father up into the air in its fear."

Tears poured freely from Millie, and her chest was rising and falling rapidly, almost gasping as she spoke. "My mother died two days later of internal injuries. My father, my distinguished father who'd given his life to heal and help others, was thought never to walk again for his legs were so mangled. He proved them wrong, but his medical career ended."

Mother Nola was gaping at her now. A look of horror or disgust, Millie wasn't sure, but she was determined to finish.

"So you see, life can change in an instant. All of your wealth could be taken away. Needed to pay for your survival. You might be forced to take work that is beneath you or not what you want to do, simply to provide for your loved ones. While I pray you never experience that, and Winston and I never experience it, it's a fact, and something you shouldn't look down on others for. Who knows, perhaps one day you will not be so high and mighty, and also be looked down upon. Only then might someone of *your class* truly understand the unfairness of it."

Millie pushed past her mother-in-law and ran up the stairs. Going to her room, she flung herself on the chair near the window and cried. She freed the tears for her mother, her father, over her hurts and sorrows. She wasn't sure how much time had passed, but the sun was sinking lower.

Sniffling, Millie managed to pull herself together, wash her face, and smooth back her hair. She returned to the parlor to retrieve her book, planning to spend the rest of her time in her bedroom until Winston came home. She had no desire to speak to Mother Nola again.

Hurt still filled her, and she moved quickly, hoping not to see her. Entering the parlor, Millie spotted her book where she'd left it and picked it up.

A movement outside the window caught her attention, and she sucked in a breath. There, through the lacy front curtains, she saw the same man she had seen earlier. This time, there was no mistaking it. He was slowly walking away, staring at the house.

Chapter 8

Winston pushed open the door and dropped his travel bag. It was good to be home. Even better, after such a long journey. He and Dr. Hudson were able to catch an early train, and he was looking forward to surprising Millie.

"You are home! And—oh! Flowers! Are those for me?" his mother asked as she hurried over with a smile on her face.

"Yes," Winston said, offering the smaller of the two bouquets he held. "And these others are for Millie." He didn't miss the twist of her mouth. While he'd known that would happen, and truly had debated getting both women the same size and type of flowers, he wanted Millie to feel special and apologize for leaving her alone so long.

Hesitating, he asked, "I hope that the two of you managed over the last week?"

"Of course we did," his mother answered, waving her hand dismissively. "Why wouldn't we?" She leaned over to sniff the mixed bouquet. "I do love purple. Thank you, Winston dear."

There were footsteps on the stairs, and Millie appeared with a smile. "Winston! You are home early. This is a wonderful surprise! I wasn't expecting you until this evening."

She hurried down the stairs and right into his arms. Winston held her tightly for a moment before pulling back enough to look down at her. "Yes, I missed you so much I couldn't stay away another moment. We just happened to catch the earlier train."

"I'm so glad," she said, nuzzled into him. "I have missed you."

Winston handed her the flowers he'd bought for her at the train station and watched as she buried her face into the soft rose petals. Clearing his throat, he asked, "Did...did everything go well?"

Millie hesitated, freezing for a moment before raising her face. "As well as could be expected, I guess."

He nodded.

"I'm glad you are home. I didn't care for being alone so long." She looked distressed, and it pulled on his heart.

"I will make it up to you then," Winston said. "We will dine out tonight."

"Really?"

Millie's face did what he had hoped. It lit up, and all traces of worry vanished.

"Yes."

"I can hardly wait," she said, clasping her hands.

"Does that invitation extend to your mother, as well?" his mother asked.

Winston had forgotten she was there. He didn't miss the look that came over Millie's face, nor the small, sad nod. She was leaving it up to him. Winston hated to tell his mother no. He knew it had been difficult for her the last few years being alone. It likely felt just as lonely at times, being here with him and Millie and perhaps feeling as though she had no place of her own in his household.

"I'm sure it does," Millie answered for him, slipping her arm into his and giving his mother a warm smile. "For you are part of our family as well."

This time, the strange look passed over his mother's face, and Winston wondered what had happened in his absence.

"I will be ready," his mother answered. "Thank you, both."

She turned and left, and Winston whispered, "Are you sure, my darling? I can tell her no."

"It's fine," Millie said. She shrugged. "I cannot blame her for missing you. I know I did. It will be a treat to hear all you did and saw. I imagine your mother also wants to know."

"You'll hear every word," he promised. Winston yawned. "Forgive me. I'm exhausted. I didn't sleep well the last few days." He didn't want to tell her why. Millie was more than capable, he knew that, but in his tired state, he didn't want to make it sound as though he didn't think she could care for herself and the house, or manage to avoid his mother's barbs.

"Why don't you rest for a while?" Millie suggested. "There's nothing urgent that needs your attention."

He hesitated. The idea sounded appealing, but he'd just come home.

"Go on," she insisted. "Perhaps I'll go visit Papa. I'll come back in a few hours."

Feeling too tired to argue, he nodded and kissed her cheek. A few hours later, while dressing for dinner, Winston had to agree Millie had been right. A little rest had been just what he needed. He felt more at ease than he had for a week.

Once the ladies were ready, the three of them took a hired carriage to his favorite restaurant. Winston relaxed inside of the carriage, listening to the rhythm of the horses' hooves. It was good to be home, and his mother and Millie seemed to be getting along better.

Millie kept her gaze out the window and Winston couldn't help but keep his eyes trained on her. Not a day passed that he didn't internally thank Aunt Rosemary for suggesting Millie as his bride. She was the perfect choice for him. His life felt complete now.

Now and again, she'd catch him looking at her and smiled before returning to the scenery beyond. At one point, she frowned, and followed something with her eyes, leaning a bit to watch where they'd been.

"What do you see?" Winston asked, stretching his neck to find what it was that had caught her attention.

"It sounds crazy, I know, but I thought I saw a man who..." She stopped.

"What man?" he asked.

"I don't know," Millie answered. "I'd not had a chance to tell you, and truthfully, I'd forgotten until just now. But while you were gone, several times I saw the same man nearby. It seemed as though he was watching the house."

Winston felt concerned. "Do you recall what he looked like?"

She nodded. "Yes. He wears an older coat that's gray, and his hat is always pulled down so far you can't see any of his face. I know that's not much of a description, but it's all I could see."

"I'm sure it was either a coincidence or else your imagination, dear," his mother answered.

Winston startled, as did Millie. His mother had never called her dear. Nor sounded so polite. Millie's eyes were wide, and she looked at Winston, as if to ask if he'd heard what happened.

The carriage pulled up then, and all thoughts of her comment ended. Winston decided to talk more about it with Millie later. His mother could be right, in that it was her imagination. Or perhaps it was even a patient, eager to see when he would reopen and was simply reading the sign he'd posted with his hours.

Yet, as they started to walk into the building, Winston felt a prickling sensation on the back of his neck. He turned slightly, and thought he saw a man watching them.

He wore an older gray coat and had his hat pulled low. When he turned fully to take in a better observation, the man was hurrying away.

A sickening jolt went through Winston. Could it be someone was following them? Was his family in danger?

Chapter 9

"Millie, have you seen where I put my pen?" Winston asked. "I've looked everywhere."

"You had it this morning. I recall you were writing something down when you were in the kitchen," she answered.

"I must have left it there," Winston said, and strode toward the door leading to the house. Just then, the office door opened and a young mother with a crying toddler entered.

"Don't worry, I'll look for it," Millie said. "You see to your patient." She quickly went into the house and found the pen, right on the kitchen counter where she'd seen it last. She turned to head back when the front door opened and closed.

Curious, Millie went to the front window. Mother Nola was leaving the house. She wondered where she was going. Regardless, at least it meant this morning she wouldn't be pulled away to make tea or put cookies on a plate or some other sort of nonsense that the woman was perfectly capable of doing on her own.

Millie was turning away when she caught sight of a man passing the window. He was in a gray coat, slowly walking behind Mother Nola.

She tensed. Should she rush outside? Millie hurried to the front door and opened it, then froze. The man was talking to Mother Nola, and she didn't seem bothered by it at all. In fact...she was smiling at him.

Filled with surprise, Millie stepped backward and closed the door. She decided to ask her about it later. Winston needed his pen, and she didn't sense any sort of danger. But still, it seemed odd. Her mother-in-law wasn't the sort to just talk to the *lower class*, as she called them. Especially to a man.

And smile? The woman almost never smiled. In fact, Millie wasn't even sure that she could. So, why was she smiling at this man?

Perhaps he was asking for directions? Or was a tradesman? They were a good neighborhood. While they lived in a nice home, it was older and someone on the street was always having some sort of repair done. Any moment, it would be their turn.

She squinted at the man for a moment through the curtain. They were still talking, though had moved behind a tree. He did appear to be the one who she kept seeing. Perhaps he had a good reason for being so near to their house. It was important not to jump to conclusions. But she'd definitely be asking Mother Nola about him when she came home.

The rest of the day was set at a frantic pace. Millie ended up staying in the clinic the whole day, and was exhausted by the time the office closed. Tiredly, she put away the last of the patient files and went into the house. Winston was still in his office, finishing with a patient.

Millie headed for the kitchen and a cup of tea. The housekeeper was making dinner and smiled at her. "You look worn out."

"I am," Millie said. "I'm so grateful you are here to help us. Dinner smells wonderful."

"Roasted chicken and vegetables," the housekeeper said. Then she asked, "Will the other Mrs. Fulton be joining us? I've not seen her today."

Millie paused, her cup of tea halfway to her lips. "Mother Nola isn't here?"

"I don't think so," the housekeeper answered as she opened the oven to check the meal. "Usually, she'd have asked for a dozen things by now. But it's been quiet."

"I wonder where—" Millie stopped as the front door opened, then closed. Footsteps sounded in the foyer. A few moments later, Mother Nola came down the hallway and strode past the kitchen's open door.

"I guess that answers that," the housekeeper said with a shrug. "Won't be long now," she added, gesturing to the oven.

Millie nodded, and with a yawn left the kitchen to refresh herself before dinner. When one was tired, there was nothing so nice as a clean face and hands to perk up a bit.

When she went up the stairs, Winston was there, changing into a clean set of clothes. He was particular—and she was grateful for it—about changing his clothing after seeing the day's patients.

"Dinner is almost ready," Millie told him.

"Good. I'm quite hungry," he said. "What a day!"

"It appears your mother had one as well," Millie said, dampening a cloth and dabbing at her face. "She's only just gotten home."

"Really? I wonder where she went. Maybe tea with a friend. Usually, though, she'd mention that the night before."

"Especially when she visits Ceclia's mother," Millie added dryly.

Winston laughed. "Yes. Have I told you yet today how glad I am I married you, and not someone else? Especially Ceclia?"

Laughing herself, Millie smiled up at him. "I'll always happily hear you say that, but yes, you have. Just now."

"Well, I am." Winston kissed her, then yawned. "Forgive me. It's not your company."

Millie nodded as her own yawn escaped. "I won't be much company myself tonight at dinner," she said. "The day has quite worn me out. I didn't even do half the work you did!"

"Mother will talk for us both," Winston said with a wink. "She won't notice at all."

But she didn't. In fact, most of dinner was quiet, something that surprised Millie. She tried, politely, to inquire about Mother Nola's day, but each question was answered shortly, or not at all.

It was obvious Winston noticed her strange manner as well, for he then asked his own questions.

"Goodness, you two are certainly a nosy lot," his mother grumbled, stabbing at her cherry tart with a fork. "If you are missing the news that much, go read a paper. What am I? The village gossip?"

"Of course not," Winston said. "We just hoped your day went well. We haven't seen you, what with being in the office all day."

"It did. Now, is there more you need to know? Or will that suffice?" his mother scowled. She rose from the table after pushing away the dessert. "If you'll excuse me, I'll retire. Perhaps you will wait to interrogate me until later?"

Millie stared in shock as her mother-in-law left the room. "What was that about?" she asked, her eyes wide.

"I have no idea," Winston said. He looked puzzled as well. "She's acting very odd as of late."

"I agree," Millie said. She took another bite of her tart. "Perhaps she's found something to interest her, but doesn't want to share what."

"There is a lot to entertain in the city," Winston agreed. "Your father was telling me that he recently took a ride through the town and was amazed how much it has changed over the last year."

"Even our neighborhood has, just since I've been here," Millie said. Then she remembered. "I think I saw that man again today. The one with the gray coat? He was talking to your mother."

Winston frowned. "Are you sure it was him?"

"As sure as I can be."

"I wonder what he wanted," Winston mused. "It can't have been important—or threatening—or else Mother would have said."

"I thought the same," Millie agreed. "Just... it's odd. I wonder if that had anything to do with how she was acting at dinner."

Winston opened his mouth to answer when there was an urgent knock on the door. He rose, and when Millie heard him say, "I'll get my bag," she rushed to fetch it.

"Here you are," she said breathlessly, meeting him in the hall as he was shrugging his coat on.

"Thank you," he said, kissing her quickly.

"Is everything alright?"

When he hesitated, her heart sped up. "Tell me," Millie whispered.

"It's...a carriage accident," Winston said.

She nodded. So that was why he hadn't wanted to tell her. For fear of upsetting her and bringing back memories from her past. Tears pricked her eyes, but Millie simply held up his doctor's bag. "Be careful."

"I will be," he told her, and then rushed out into the night.

As the door shut, Mother Nola came down the stairs. "What is all the commotion?" she asked. "I heard shouting in the streets from upstairs." She went to the window to peer out.

"There's been a carriage accident," Millie said softly.

His mother glanced at her, and seemed to sense Millie's distress. Then, to her surprise, she walked closer and rested a hand on her arm. "I'm sure all will be well, and Winston will return safe," she said quietly.

The unexpected kindness nearly spilled the tears Millie was holding back. So, she simply nodded, and hurried upstairs. Once there, she peered through the window, hoping to see some sign of Winston. There was none.

Letting out a shuddering sob, she knelt and prayed that indeed, Winston would return to her safely, but that the others involved in the accident would also remain safe. She wouldn't wish the pain she and her father had felt over the years on anyone.

Millie wiped her eyes, then waited downstairs in the parlor. Sleep wouldn't come to her, nor any sort of relaxation, until Winston was home safe.

Mother Nola joined her in the silent vigil, and the two sat, books in hand, but neither doing more than looking through the window to the dark street.

Rain fell, beating lightly against the glass pane. Tiny droplets caught the lamplight and sparkled as they dripped downward. A draft came from the window, and Millie wondered if Winston was warm enough.

Every now and then, Millie would flick her eyes toward Winston's mother. She wondered why she was there. Was it simply her worry over Winston? Or was it something more? Mother Nola rarely seemed rattled or flustered. Even now, she sat calmly. Stoic, even. So, why was she here? Especially after she'd been so upset at dinner.

The thought came to her then. Was Mother Nola there because of her? Could that be?

The front door opened before Millie could sit with that thought, and she rushed over as Winston came in, damp with the rain. "You're back," she sighed in relief as she took his coat.

"Yes. And everyone is well, and alive, and relatively uninjured," he told her with a smile. "Nothing more than bumps, bruises, and minor lacerations."

"That makes me feel better," Millie sighed.

"You shouldn't have waited up," Winston said, setting his bag down. "I know how tired you were." His eyes filled with concern. "Were you lonely here all by yourself?"

"Oh no," Millie said. She glanced behind her to where Winston's mother likely was. "I was..."

But Mother Nola was nowhere to be seen. Where had she gone?

Winston was walking to the kitchen. "Tea and bed for me," he said. "Luckily it didn't start to rain until I was on the way home." He continued talking, but Millie didn't hear him. She was feeling too confused, as she looked at the top of the stairs, where a soft click signaled Mother Nola's door closing.

Chapter 10

Winston finished the last of his coffee and set his napkin on the table. "I'll be in the office," he said.

"I'll join you shortly," Millie told him, looking up from her toast and jam. "I'm almost done."

"There's no rush," he told her. "You know I like to be there early to be sure everything is set up. I also need to reset my bag from last night's incident. I was so tired, I didn't replace my supplies or clean my instruments." He checked his pocketwatch. "Your father will actually be here in about an hour, as well."

"Oh really?" Millie's face brightened. "He does love working in the office."

"I see no reason why he shouldn't," Winston said. He added, "It's nice to have another physician there. I wonder if he'd ever consider becoming partners."

His wife's broad smile was all he needed to put a skip into his step as he moved to the door separating the house and the office. Winston unlocked the door from the house side and stepped into the waiting room.

Dim light from a crack in the curtains illuminated his way. He reached the first window, pulled back the curtains and went for the second. As he drew that curtain away and turned around, he froze.

Millie's desk drawer was open. It was always kept shut. He walked over, pushed it closed and, with a sudden feeling of worry filling him, hurried to the back room where he saw patients.

The room was in disarray. The crate where he kept bandages had been knocked over. Medical supplies and instruments lay on the floor. The cabinet with wound care and some small jars of medicine had been opened. Bottles were on their sides and a quick glance told him several were missing.

Winston rushed to the supply room. When he opened it, he staggered. The room had been rummaged through. At first glance, he couldn't tell how much was damaged or was missing, only that it was obvious both had happened. Broken glass filled the floor, liquids and powders were mixed in, and storage boxes had been opened, their contents upended.

The door between the house and office rattled and slowly creaked open.

Millie. What if the thief was still here?

"Get in the house," Winston shouted, sure she'd heard him. "Lock the door."

The door closed quickly, then there was a click. He allowed himself a moment of relief before he pulled open the office door leading to the outside.

He ran to the front door, where Millie stood, alarm on her face. "I've got to fetch the police," he told her. "Someone's broken into the office."

Millie's face paled. "Go ahead. I'll stop patients from going in."

Winston hated to risk her being in danger. But she was right. They must stop them. Just then, a policeman walked past, whistling.

"Wait!" Winston called to the officer. He turned to Millie. "Send the housekeeper to get a carriage to fetch your father."

When she nodded, he turned to the officer, who drew close. "Someone's broken into my medical office."

The officer tensed. "Are they still there?"

"Not that I saw. But..." Winston hesitated. "I only looked briefly in the rooms, then ran to get help."

"Smart man." The officer looked around a moment, presumably for a colleague or sign of the intruder. "Wait here. I'll investigate."

Winston did as he was told. A few minutes later, a carriage came at a fast speed, and he saw the face of Millie's father through the closed window, looking concerned.

As he helped his father-in-law out of the carriage, Winston hurriedly explained. "Someone broke into the office. I'm going to get my ledger to see who we were to attend to today. I'll be able to see most patients at their homes. But I don't want to leave Millie or my mother alone. And as patients come, I need someone to explain they must leave."

"You can count on me," Dr. Hudson answered. "Are you and Millie hurt? Your mother? The housekeeper? When did it happen?"

"It must have happened in the middle of the night. We are all fine. Just...the office." Winston shook his head. He still felt a shock over the incident. There was a sense of unease now, thinking about the fact someone so easily, and uncaringly, broke into the office.

The policeman came just then. "You were robbed, alright. No one else is inside. I'm going to go get another policeman. We have someone who investigates. He'll ask you questions and poke around. Please don't go back inside until he gets here."

"May I go into my home?" Winston asked.

"Yes, just not the office," the policeman said. "I'll be back in an hour or less."

Winston nodded. He and Dr. Hudson walked to the house's front door, where Millie and his mother stood anxiously.

"The office was broken into," Winston explained, thinking it best to start at the beginning. "The police have taken a fast look to make sure the thief isn't still there. They'll be back shortly to look around further and ask questions."

"How terrible," Millie said, dismay on her face. "How bad does it look? Is there much damage?"

"Why would anyone want to break into your office?" his mother asked. "It doesn't make sense."

"Likely for medicines," Winston sighed, running his hand over his jaw. "It's obvious several are missing, but until I can get in there to look everything over and get it back in order, I won't be able to tell just what or how much."

Dr. Hudson shook his head. "It's a terrible thing. Let me know how I can help you."

"Your assistance with my patients who may still arrive will be invaluable," Winston said. "I truly could not do this without your help."

"It might be a long morning," Millie said. "I'll help the housekeeper with tea and some sort of refreshment for everyone, including whatever officers come."

Winston nodded. That was a good idea, and not something he'd have thought of himself. He was glad for Millie's clear-headedness.

There was a loud knock, startling everyone, and Winston opened the door to the officers. After he, Dr. Hudson, and the lawmen toured the office and answered questions, they returned to the house.

Millie offered tea, coffee, and an assortment of cookies, which the two policemen eagerly helped themselves to.

"We'd like to speak with you ladies as well," the first officer, who identified himself as Officer Holmes said.

"I'm afraid I didn't hear a thing," the housekeeper said, twisting her hands.

"The same goes for me," his mother said. "It was a terrible shock when Winston told us. Crime, in this neighborhood? You will improve your watch, won't you?"

"Of course," the second officer, Investigator Jones said. He looked at Millie.

"What of you, Mrs. Fulton? Did you hear or see anything that might be helpful?"

Millie hesitated, which made both officers lean forward. The investigator pulled out his notepad. "I've noticed a man hanging about," she admitted. "I told Winston about him."

"That's right!" Winston said. He smacked the table with his hand. "I saw him too, the night we all went out for dinner. But when I turned to get a better look, he vanished."

"Yes, and I observed him talking to Mother Nola," Millie said. "Just the other day." She bit her lip. "Could he have been the thief?"

"Of course not," his mother snapped. "You and your overactive imagination."

Winston looked at her carefully. She seemed flustered. Her face had turned pink. "Who was the man you were talking to?" he asked.

"It was nothing. He...he was asking for directions," his mother said. "My goodness. You seek to blame that innocent man?"

"We don't know that he's innocent," Officer Holmes said. "That's why we are asking. Can you tell me what he looks like?"

Millie looked at him, but Winston shrugged. "I've never seen his face."

"I've only seen him from a distance," Millie said. "He wears an older gray coat. It's clean, though worn. He's got a hat that matches, but he's always got it low over his face, or else he's a bit in the shadows and I can't see what he looks like beyond that."

"And you, Mrs. Fulton?" the investigator asked, looking at his mother. "You spoke with him. Can you give us a description?"

"I...ah...no, er...that is," Winston's mother shook her head. "I wasn't paying attention. I was in a hurry, heading to tea. At Cecilia's mother's house." She pressed her lips together.

"Alright then," the investigator said. "We'll ask some neighbors and look around. Once you get the place back to rights, give us a list of what's missing. That may also help."

"I will," Winston said.

"Do you...do you think the person will come back?" Millie asked.

Winston could hear the touch of fear in her voice and moved closer to her. He put his arm around her shoulders to comfort her and she leaned into him. He hated that she was frightened, and vowed not to leave her side.

"I doubt it," the investigator assured her. "He likely got what he wanted and has moved on. We'll keep the place under watch as well."

"Thank you," Winston said, standing. "I'll show you out."

He walked the policemen to the door. As he returned and went into the office to start cleaning up the mess, he glanced out the window. His mother was hurrying down the street, her head twisting this way and that.

Why had she left? Was it to tell her friends what had happened? It seemed odd that she was going out alone, after what had just happened. Winston replayed her reactions over in his mind. He felt quite concerned she knew something—if not about the theft, then about the man with the gray coat. What was she hiding?

Chapter 11

Millie finished copying the list of the medical supplies they needed to replace. One copy was for the police investigator, another for the store to get the supplies, and the original would stay there in the office, so the items could be checked off one at a time as they were replaced.

While thankfully not much had been stolen, a good number of things had been dirtied or damaged. In the supply room, several glass jars that held supplies had been knocked over and shattered. It had taken the better part of a day to set things to rights.

Stretching, Millie stood. She needed one more sheet of paper to send a note along with the list, so the investigator knew what it was.

She walked to the parlor, where a small desk sat near the window. There would be some in there. As she entered, she saw Mother Nola leaned over the desk, writing.

"I don't mean to disturb you," Millie said, drawing closer. "I just need a piece of paper." When there was no answer, she stepped closer. "Mother Nola?"

The woman jumped. "What do you want?" she asked, turning over the paper she'd been writing on. Then she hurriedly covered up an envelope that was nearby.

Millie pretended not to notice the sudden movements. "I need one more piece of paper," she said. "Also, an envelope, please, so I can get this list sent over to the police investigator for Winston."

Wordlessly, Mother Nola handed over the items and stared at her, a look of impatience on her face. Millie turned, trying not to sneak glances at her mother-in-law. This was just another of the things to add to the list of odd occurrences.

A short while later, she returned to the parlor, and Mother Nola was gone. There was a book she didn't recognize sitting on the table near the window. Millie picked it up, curious. Just then, some flying insect whizzed past her, and Millie waved her hand to swat it away. However, she accidently dropped the book.

When she stooped to pick it up, there was something sticking out of it. Millie rose, then opened the book. Her eyes widened. Inside were several envelopes, all addressed to Mother Nola. The handwriting wasn't feminine, and there was no return address. She wanted to open one of the envelopes to see the contents, but hurried footsteps on the stairs alerted her and she returned the book, then swiftly sat at the desk, taking out a sheet of paper as though she were writing.

Mother Nola strode in, snatched the book, and left without a word or a backward glance. Millie frowned and rose from the desk. What was going on?

The front door opened, and Millie stood at the edge of the window. She watched as Mother Nola went outside and across the street. The man in the gray coat was there! They talked for only a moment, then Mother Nola hurried back to this side of the street. The man in gray, however, stuffed something into his coat pocket. Was it an envelope? Had it been whatever Mother Nola was writing when Millie had interrupted her?

Millie bit her lip. Mother Nola had a great deal of money from her first marriage. Could it be she was being threatened? Blackmailed? In most circumstances, Millie would have laughed at herself, but she also knew Mother Nola was quite concerned with appearances. Perhaps she said or did something that could potentially ruin her reputation and was trying to protect it. Such things did happen. Was the office break in a warning to Mother Nola to cooperate?

The idea was likely preposterous. Still, she knew she must tell Winston. But would he think she was imagining things?

Though her mother-in-law had been unkind to her on more than a few occasions, she was still family. She was important to Winston, and that made Mother Nola important to Millie.

But maybe she should ask her mother-in-law first. Maybe if she was in trouble, she wanted to keep it private. She wasn't quite sure what to do, but Millie wanted to make sure Mother Nola wasn't in danger somehow.

Their relationship was confusing. Most of the time, Mother Nola didn't treat her kindly. But then, there were the few times she did. Like when Winston had gone to assist the carriage accident. The thing that confused Millie the most was that her mother-in-law, on occasion, did show kindness. The rest of the time it was secrecy, or unkindness. That didn't stop her from being concerned, though.

Millie might not be friends with Mother Nola, but they were family. And she wanted to protect her or help her if she needed it.

She walked to the foyer, intending to find Winston to talk to, and came face to face with Mother Nola just as she walked in. The other woman tried to walk past her, but Millie blocked her. She felt nervous asking, but she had to do it. Had to know.

Taking a deep breath, Millie blurted, "Are you in trouble?"

Her mother-in-law gave her a strange look. "Whatever are you talking about? The fact you are here? Yes, it's troublesome. But, I bear it. One day, you too might have a daughter-in-law you must live with."

Millie pressed her lips together. Leave it to the woman to take every opportunity to say something unkind. Especially when she was only trying to help.

"No, I meant the man outside." She crossed her arms. "I saw you hand him something and he hurried away. I also know that's the man you've spoken to before. The man Winston saw when we went to dinner. The man I have seen on several occasions watching the house. The man who, possibly, was responsible for the thefts in Winston's office."

Mother Nola gasped, and fury filled her face. "He was not. How dare you?"

"I dare," Mille said, "because it's obvious you know something about this man you aren't telling us or the investigator. How do you know him? How are you sure he had nothing to do with Winston's office being broken into, and things damaged and stolen?"

"What I know, what I do, and who I talk to is none of your business." Mother Nola's voice was low. "Perhaps you should spend your time minding your husband's business, like he wants you to, and stay out of mine."

Millie drew herself to her full height and said, "I'm done with you bullying me. You aren't going to tell me what to do any longer." She stepped closer to her mother-in-law and softened her voice. "Is it so hard for you to imagine that I am worried about you? For you? Winston and I care about you very much. You are his mother, and mine now as well. You might not want to tell me if you are in trouble, but I promise I'm going to get to the bottom of this and find out who that man is. The reason being is that I am worried about you and want to help you if you need it. I only hope we are still cordial to one another after I do."

Chapter 12

An air of tension had filled the house for the last several days. Millie and his mother made a point to avoid each other as much as possible. When in the same room, they tried not to talk to the other, though Millie made more of an effort to be polite than his mother did.

Winston was tired of it. It was foolish behavior. What was worse was he had no idea why his mother was so upset. He decided it was time to sit down with both his mother and Millie, and get the situation resolved.

At the same time, though he knew it was a good idea, he was also concerned it might make the situation worse.

Rising from his desk, he took a deep breath and went through the house looking for them. He didn't have to look very hard. He could hear them from the kitchen.

"...my tea. You know—"

"Mother." Winston stood there in the kitchen doorway, and took in the scene before him.

Millie looked upset and had tears in her eyes. His mother was red-faced and angry. Winston sighed. He hated to be in the middle of the two of them. He loved each, and while Millie never asked him to choose sides and she was always kind, he knew she was tired of this as much as he was.

"Mother, please stop," Winston said quietly. "You've done enough, you've said enough. It's time for you to stop. Since you aren't happy here, perhaps you'd like to move elsewhere. Think about what you'd like to do, and let me know."

Her expression was one of shock, so was Millie's. Before anyone could say a thing, there was a crash.

"The office?" Millie asked, fear in her eyes.

"Wait here," Winston said, and moved toward the door leading to the office. He stopped though, when shouts from outside drew his attention. A man was running, chasing after a child.

Winston opened the door and looked out. Neighbors had gathered at the house next door, where a broken window was the focus of their attention. He went back in, quickly checked the office, and returned to Millie.

"It was next door. A broken window by a child."

She sagged in relief. "Thank goodness. I'm so worried the person will return."

"I'm sure they won't," Winston said. "The officers didn't seem to think so." He wanted to believe that as well, but admittedly, the fear the individual would return was in the back of his mind too.

He looked over at Millie. "Everything will be okay. Of that I am sure. The person will be caught."

She nodded, though she wore the same doubtful look he felt. Millie suddenly glanced around. "Where is your mother?"

"I don't know," he said, in surprise, twisting his neck to look around. "Wasn't she just here?"

"She has been sneaking out a lot," Millie said.

The sound of the front door opening and closing caught his attention.

Pressing her lips together, Millie said, "This time, I'm going to follow her."

"Millie..."

"I want to know, Winston. She knows something about that man. What if she's in trouble? Being blackmailed? Threatened? What if he's the one who broke into the office? She won't tell us, so I want to find out. If something is wrong, we need to help her. Even if she doesn't want us to."

Millie hurried into the foyer. "I'll be careful," she promised. "Papa will be here soon. He can help with the patients."

Then, she slipped out of the door. Winston hurried to the window. His heart nearly stopped. There, walking down the street, was his mother, a man in a gray coat following her.

About a dozen paces behind him, followed Millie. As she passed the house, she nodded toward the window, as if she knew he was there.

Winston wanted to join her. He was sorely tempted to leave his patients to her father, but sighed. He had to be responsible. He also had to trust that Millie would be careful.

If this man in gray was a danger, he couldn't live with himself if she was hurt in some way.

Chapter 13

Millie stayed well behind Mother Nola and the strange man who was following her. Mother Nola took a path that weaved this way and that, and didn't seem to lead to any one place. Millie was starting to feel lost, but finally, after her legs were starting to tire, Mother Nola led them to a large park.

Still following, Millie hung back, keeping trees and large bushes between herself, Mother Nola, and the mysterious man. She was nervous they might spot her, and hoped so far they hadn't. Sneaking around wasn't something she'd ever done before, and knew it would be just her bad luck to trip or sneeze or something and draw attention to herself.

Eventually, after passing several flower beds, Mother Nola sat on a bench. Not a moment later, the man came toward her. Millie wondered if he would pass by, but to her immense surprise, the man sat next to her mother-in-law.

Millie watched closely. They were talking, that much was obvious, but she was too far away to hear what they were saying. She was also unsure of their expressions, as their backs were to her.

Impatiently, she waited about a half hour, then started walking again, following the pair as they continued through the park. Mother Nola and the man went into a small café. Millie paced back and forth unsure of what to do. She couldn't enter. They'd see her. So, she waited. Almost an hour later, they exited, talking with their heads close.

Millie strained to hear as she followed them. Their voices were too low and she had to hang back as to not be spotted. She wondered if the investigator who was looking into Winston's office robbery ever had to trail someone. If he did, how did he do it? It was terribly difficult.

The man and Mother Nola continued to walk. Unfortunately, since she was behind them, she still couldn't see their expressions or have any clue at all about what was happening or being said.

This was confusing. Mother Nola didn't appear to feel threatened.

A carriage pulled alongside them, and Mother Nola climbed into it, the man following.

"Great. Now what? I can't follow on foot," Millie fretted, looking in each direction for another carriage. There was none.

As the carriage left, she watched it, feeling irritated. She had no answers for all of her trouble. What she had now were even more questions. Why were they in the carriage? Was Mother Nola being forced to go somewhere?

She didn't have that impression, but wasn't sure if she should look for a policeman or not. Should she go back and get Winston? But what would she tell him? She had no firm facts or clues.

With a sigh, Millie headed back to the house and the office. She was slower on foot. She'd been in such a hurry, she forgot to take her handbag and had no money for a transportation fare. It was just as well there hadn't been another carriage.

Her feet were throbbing now, and Millie longed to sit for a while. She was tired and thirsty after walking all over. Coming upon her street, she sped up slightly, anxious to get home. There was no reason to slink about and lurk in shadows. She lived here. Besides, she'd lost whatever direction Mother Nola and the mysterious man had gone.

The fact she was with him bothered Millie greatly. Just this morning, the newspaper had a story of an elderly widow who had been tricked out of her money by an unscrupulous man. While Mother Nola wasn't exactly elderly, she was wealthy. Was she also easily flattered? Millie wasn't sure. If so, had this man flattered her in some way? She had been smiling at him.

Millie's eyes narrowed. If only she'd been able to hear what they were saying. The last few hours had been a waste. Instead of being able to share with Winston—and possibly the police investigator—what she'd learned, she had nothing but more questions.

Turning onto the street where their home was located, she couldn't help but feel relief. These really hadn't been the proper shoes to wear for so much walking. Once she returned home, she was making tea and putting her feet up.

The house was in sight now, and Millie wondered if there were still patients in the office.

There was a movement, and just three houses away she stopped in surprise as the man in the gray coat appeared. She hurried closer. He was...leaving their house? His long stride carried him in the opposite direction.

Her legs wouldn't move any faster, but Millie could be sure the man hadn't been in the office, he'd been inside the house.

He was hurrying away, and Millie watched in alarm. Something worrying was happening, but she didn't know what.

Millie entered the house. Mother Nola was on the stairs. She looked at Millie, then looked away.

"Did I see a man leaving here, just now?" Millie asked.

"I don't know what you are talking about," Mother Nola said, with her usual sniff.

Millie crossed her arms over her chest. "Yes, you do. Remember what I said. I'll figure it out."

There was no answer as Mother Nola climbed the stairs, pointedly ignoring her. Millie took a deep breath. No matter she had so little to go on. She was going to figure this out. It was simply a matter of time.

Her aching feet forgotten, Millie went into Winston's office. The door was closed to the examination room, and his voice muffled through the door. He must be with a patient.

She sat at her desk and checked the list of patients to be seen. He had one more after this. While she was impatient to tell him about the time she'd spent following Mother Nola, and the man who'd been with her, she also knew there was nothing much to say. Would he even be interested?

Millie took up the broom and swept the waiting room floor, then straightened the chairs. She had to keep busy, or else she'd be too tempted to interrupt Winston, even though she had little to share.

A short time later, the front office door opened at the same time Winston emerged from the examination room. He smiled at Millie, then raised his eyebrows as if to ask had she learned anything. Millie gave a small shrug, and he helped the next patient into the room to be treated.

Luckily for her, he wasn't there long as it was simply a follow-up on the woman's hand laceration.

When the last patient had left, Millie assisted Winston in cleaning the examination room, and filled him in on her adventure.

"How does Mother know him?" Winston mused. "And why wouldn't she admit that she did?"

"It bothers me too," Millie said. "That's why I'm terribly worried that perhaps she's being blackmailed or he's trying to weasel himself into her purse."

"You are a wonderful daughter-in-law," Winston told her, giving her an admiring look. "You are also an incredible and thoughtful wife. I know Mother's not been kind to you, I also know she's been very difficult to get along with, yet you do it splendidly."

Millie smiled up at him. "Of course. She's family. We might not always like our family members, after all, we didn't get to choose them, but we can still treat them kindly, with respect, and concern." She sighed heavily then. "I just hope, desperately, that if she is in any trouble, she will let us know before it goes too far."

"I hope she will as well," Winston said, with a small frown. He shook his head. "Mother is proud. Sometimes too proud."

At his words, a chill came over Millie. She rubbed her arms and felt the goosebumps. What would happen to

Mother Nola if she continued to keep this secret and she was in danger? Millie didn't want to find out.

Chapter 14

Winston turned over in bed. It felt like hours now that he'd been trying to get to sleep. Frustratingly, it eluded him. His body was tired, however, his mind was not.

Had he been one of his patients, he'd have suggested the usual remedies. A mug of warm milk. Some chamomile tea. A light snack. None of those things had helped him though, for the last few nights. By this point, he was simply exhausted. And worried.

Millie was asleep, and a sliver of moonlight shone on her face, illuminating it as though she were an angel. He smiled at the thought. There was no one else who was as patient nor as kind, so perhaps she was one.

Heavenly sent, to be sure. She must be, to put up with his mother the way that she did.

Trying not to wake her, he slipped from the bed and peered out the window. Seeing nothing, but still feeling unease throughout him, he creeped through the house in his pajamas, checking each window and door to be sure they were locked.

The break in had been unsettling. That's all it was, he tried to assure himself. Yet, he wasn't entirely convinced that was the reason for his sleeplessness. Without a doubt, he knew until the person responsible for breaking into his office was caught, he'd be on guard. However, another truth was he was also worried about his mother.

What if Millie was right? Could his mother be susceptible to someone who would charm and flatter his way into her heart first, and her bank account second, leaving her penniless? Or was she being blackmailed in some way? She'd always been a private person, so the thought of either was difficult for him to fathom.

With him working so often, he supposed Millie would be the better judge of if that was a possibility. He didn't want to snoop around and ask his mother, but still... she was his mother and he worried about her wellbeing and her happiness. Especially with her no longer having a husband to watch over her or see to her whims.

His mother was used to a particular lifestyle, one of comfort which she enjoyed. He couldn't provide that for her if something took away her financial means. Much of her wealth came from an inheritance, passed down three generations. While he was given a small portion upon his father's passing, the majority went to his mother to see for her care.

After quietly descending the stairs, Winston looked through the front window, simultaneously checking the lock. Though he'd never seen the man in the gray coat lurking before the house, Millie had described him there several times, and he half expected to see the man across the street near the trees, eyes fixed upon their house.

The police hadn't learned anything about him. So, either that meant he was a law-abiding citizen or else he wasn't from around there. They also had no luck in determining who had broken into the office. The man who had been watching the house was still a suspect, though neither the police nor Winston were sure if the man and the robbery were connected.

That in itself was most unsettling. And it made it difficult to get a good night's sleep, when one worried about another incident. He almost wished it would happen, so that he'd have a chance at catching the culprit and putting him behind bars so that he could return to his sleep undisturbed.

Someone moved outside on the darkened street, a shadow that made his heart thud. Winston swallowed hard and reached for the walking stick that was nearby. It wasn't much, but he'd be ready to protect his home and family, at whatever cost.

As the figure grew nearer the streetlamp, Winston was relieved to see it was merely a policeman, not someone intent on vandalism. True to their word, the officers had been patrolling the area. This was the first he'd seen them at night, but it filled him with relief.

Feeling better, he returned to the stairs, went down the hallway, and slid back into bed. Though he was tired, sleep still refused him. Instead, all he had was what felt like endless questions. Questions about the break in, about his mother, this strange man, and most of all, about how to see his wife and his mother not just co-exist in the home, but also to get along. Could such a thing even happen?

What he needed, he decided, was more information. Someone who knew everything about everyone to both advise him and answer those questions. But who? A smile curved on his lips as the answer came at once, and he suddenly felt much better.

While the police were the right ones for the job of discovering who had broken into his office, there was only one person who knew everything about everyone.

Aunt Rosemary.

Yes. He'd visit her, explain what had been happening, and see if she knew who the strange man was who had been appearing, and why his mother might be behaving so unusually. His aunt had seen and heard so much in her many years, if his mother was being blackmailed, it was likely Aunt Rosemary could find out why and by whom.

In fact, chances were very good that not only would Aunt Rosemary know what was happening, if she didn't, she'd likely find the information far faster than he, Millie, or even the police could do. There was little Aunt Rosemary didn't know, but her network was expansive, and she'd be able to help him. He felt sure of it.

The fact that they were family would make Aunt Rosemary even more invested in helping discover the truth of the matter. The woman would brook no scandal touching her, and if there was even so much as a whiff of something unsavory, she'd discover it and quickly find a remedy.

Winston turned over and let his gaze wander through the window to the night sky. Perhaps in just a few days this would all be behind him, and he'd be able to sleep soundly again at night.

Perhaps.

One problem at a time.

Chapter 15

Breakfast the next morning was a calm affair. Mother Nola didn't come down to join them, instead requesting a tray to her room. Millie happily obliged, then hurried back to Winston, who looked exhausted. She knew he'd been having trouble sleeping soundly after the break in, and it worried her.

"Papa is on his way," Millie said. "The carriage was sent for him. Do you want to go back to bed and sleep for a while?"

"No, but I do want you to go with me somewhere," Winston said.

"Oh? Where to?" Millie asked, surprised.

Winston looked around for a moment to be sure they were alone, then leaned in closely. "To see Aunt Rosemary."

Millie furrowed her brow. "Aunt Rosemary?"

"Yes." Winston leaned back in his chair, a pleased expression on his face. "I thought of it last night."

"I'm afraid I don't understand," Millie said, shaking her head. "How can Aunt Rosemary help? Actually, I suppose my question should be, why do you want her help?"

Winston explained, "You see, Aunt Rosemary knows an extraordinary amount about everyone and everything. What she doesn't know, well, she'll know who to ask."

Millie understood then. At least, she thought she did. "So you are going to ask her about the man in the gray jacket?"

"I am." He wore a grin.

"The police, even with their vast resources, have not discovered who he is. What makes you think your aunt can?" Millie asked, genuinely curious.

"I just do," Winston said. "There is not much Aunt Rosemary can't discover when she sets her mind to it." He took a bite of his toast. "That's why I asked for your father to come this morning. I really don't know how long we will be there and the patients must have care. I sent a note earlier to let Aunt Rosemary know we'd be arriving late morning, in case she's not an early riser."

"Then I will get ready," Millie said. She leaned over and kissed his cheek. "Perhaps she will have answers. I am more than curious to learn who this man is, and why your mother is pretending that she doesn't know him."

"As am I," Winston said grimly.

Millie hurried up the stairs to choose a hat. As she passed Mother Nola's door, she paused. What secrets were behind it? Were they of the good kind, or the sort that made her fear for Mother Nola's safety?

Slowly walking away, deep in thought, Millie chose her hat and handbag, then returned downstairs, just as Winston was opening the front door for her father.

"Thank you for coming," Winston said. "I'm so grateful you were able to be here, especially on such short notice."

Millie smiled. She adored how Winston always made her father feel as though he were doing him a favor. In truth, Winston likely felt that way. He was such a good man and cared so deeply for others. That's what made him an exceptional physician. She felt proud and happy at how well they got along and how the two of them worked well together.

"I'm delighted to help," her father answered, moving slowly into the foyer. "There were no classes or lectures today at the university, so the timing is quite convenient."

"I don't know how long we'll be gone," Winston said.

"There's no need to rush," her father said. He smiled at both her and Winston. "I'm well acquainted with the office and the patients. Do enjoy yourself, though. Take my daughter out for some fresh air. Perhaps around the park's garden."

Just then, there was the sound of someone on the stairs. Millie turned and saw Mother Nola. She was wearing a new striped dress, a hat Millie hadn't ever seen before, and was coolly gazing at them all.

Millie's father greeted her, and she nodded, then turned to Winston. "I am having morning tea with Ceclia's mother."

Millie noticed her father heading toward the office. He winked at her as he left.

"Do enjoy yourself," Winston said. "Tell her Millie and I said hello."

It was all Millie could do not to giggle. She nodded though, in agreement with his words.

With her usual sniff, his mother left, and Millie moved to the window.

"Any sign of the man?" Winston asked, peering across the street with her.

"No. Perhaps she really is having tea with her friend," Millie answered. Then she frowned. "Or is meeting him somewhere."

"Speaking of meeting, we should go," Winston said. He opened the door. "The carriage that brought your father is waiting for us."

"Oh, that's thoughtful of you," Millie said.

She climbed in, and Winston sat next to her. Millie let her gaze settle outside of the window. As they rode along, she observed how busy the morning seemed to be. Several times their carriage slowed with the heavy traffic of the town.

Suddenly, Millie leaned forward. "Winston, isn't that your mother?"

"Where?" Winston looked where she was pointing.

"There. She just went into the bank." Millie felt nerves rise up in her stomach. "I wonder why."

Winston called out, "Stop, please! One moment!"

The driver moved to the side of the road, and Winston jumped out. "Wait here," he said, both to Millie and the driver, then he disappeared.

Millie waited anxiously as Winston vanished into the bank. She kept her gaze focused on the door, watching for him. A short time later, he came out and shook his head. "Nothing," he told her. "I didn't see her inside, though I know she went in."

"I wonder where she went," Millie mused, leaning back against the seat. "I know I saw her."

"I did as well," Winston said. "I looked to see if she was hiding somewhere. The only other place would be if she went into a back room with the manager, like she's done before, to discuss something private. I wouldn't be permitted there." He shook his head. "Her behavior is becoming more alarming. I'm glad that we are going to see Aunt Rosemary."

"You seem so sure she can help," Millie said as they set off once more. "I do hope you are right. I am worried about your mother."

Winston's hand found hers. "She will help. Of that I am sure. I feel as certain about it as I did in knowing it was you I wanted to marry."

Millie's cheeks warmed. Winston always said the sweetest of things, and though they had been married for several months now, she never tired of hearing his thoughtful words, and hoped he'd never stop.

They sat quietly the rest of the drive, but soon arrived outside of the home where Aunt Rosemary resided. Winston climbed out of the carriage and helped her down.

"I hope she got my note," he said, as they went up the front walk. "I didn't get a reply."

"I'm sure she did," Millie said, scanning the front of the building. "It appears someone is home."

Winston knocked, and the door was opened a moment later by a woman Millie didn't recognize. As they went into the familiar parlor, Aunt Rosemary greeted them.

Her face wore an expression of distaste. Her lips were twisted, and her eyes hard. Without even greeting them, she asked, placing her hands on her hips, "Are you aware of what your mother is doing?"

Chapter 16

Winston tensed, and then fought back a wince at the greeting. "Perhaps not fully," he answered. "Hello, Aunt Rosemary. Yes, Mother is why we've come to see you. We hoped you might help us with a problem."

His aunt arched one of her brows and shook her head. With a wave of her arm, she said in that throaty voice of hers, "It's good you did. If there's a scandal, we need to stop it before it goes further." Then she looked over. "Hello, Millie dear."

"Hello, Aunt Rosemary," Millie answered, accepting the older woman's squeeze of the hand.

"Let's have tea," Aunt Rosemary said. "You will tell me what you know, I will tell you what I know." Her tone wasn't one of asking.

"Of course," Winston said.

Once they all sat, he looked at Millie. "It's hard to know where to start," he said. "And I was surprised to know just now that you've heard of something about Mother."

"Mmm. Well, I've had three people ask me this week who the shabby looking man was she had been seen with." Aunt Rosemary shook her head. "I'm expected to know things. Imagine my surprise at the questions!"

She waved her hands around. "It was most unsettling. I had to promise to tell them all about it at a later date and pretend I was late for an appointment. What a terrible situation she has put me in."

Winston kept his smile to himself. No wonder his aunt looked so distressed. She not only prided herself on knowing everything, but she also wasn't usually in the position of someone else having information she didn't. Unsettled was likely just how she felt. It was the same feeling deep within him.

He glanced at Millie. "I don't know how much we can tell you," he admitted. "That's why we are here."

"Start with what you do know," Aunt Rosemary said.

Millie glanced at him, then nervously said, "Several weeks ago, I spotted a man staring at the house. It wasn't just once. It happened often. He would stand across the street and just look at the house."

"Go on," Aunt Rosemary said, then raised her tea cup.

"It appeared that he was watching Mother Nola. But I really don't know." Millie looked over at Winston.

He nodded at her. She continued. "She was nervous when I mentioned him, and I saw the man following her. There was another time she wrote a note and gave it to him. I saw them talking, and asked her about it, but she was dismissive. Said he was asking for directions."

"And you do not think she is telling the truth?" Aunt Rosemary asked, looking at him and Millie.

"I'm not convinced she isn't," Winston said. "Mother wouldn't stop and speak with someone such as that man, unless she had reason to. You know how she feels about those who appear lower class."

His aunt nodded, then fixed her gaze on Millie. "Yes. Our mother drilled that into us as young women. Anything else?"

"I also found several letters to her from a man, hidden away in a book. She took it before I could look further." Millie looked worried. "That's when I wondered if perhaps she was being asked to give him money. We saw her go into the bank on our way here." Her cheeks turned pink and she looked into her tea. "It happens sometimes, that a woman of means and advanced age is taken advantage of and...maybe it's just a silly worry, but—"

"It's not," Aunt Rosemary said. "You are very thoughtful to be concerned. I know Nola isn't always the kindest with her words, and I've no doubt she's been rather abrasive in her speech with you. And for you to still be concerned speaks volumes of your character."

"That's what I think," Winston said with a smile at his wife.

"I knew you'd be perfect together," Aunt Rosemary said with a nod. "Just perfect. So few could handle Nola, like you, Millie."

"But then things got strange." Millie looked worried. Winston felt that way himself, but didn't want to voice that opinion.

"Go on," Aunt Rosemary ordered. Her gaze was intense, focused on Millie.

"After the break-ins, she told the investigators that she didn't know who the man was, when I mentioned seeing him. But they'd spoken together! Not long after, I followed them when I saw the man again, across the street watching the house, and Mother Nola went out to talk to him. He and Mother Nola walked quite a distance, separate, but still going to the same place."

"Fascinating," Aunt Rosemary mused. "Perhaps that's when others saw them as well. The thing I don't understand is why she wasn't being more careful. Nola has always taken care with her appearances."

"They were trying to be discreet," Millie said. "However, they were together at a park, and then they went to a café."

"Is that so?" his aunt rose and went to a bookcase, where she browsed for a moment before taking a book from the shelf.

The volume was of medium thickness, with a blue spine. After flipping through the pages, she nodded and walked over to them.

"Nola Francesca Milton Fulton. One of four, daughter of a wealthy businessman. Married at age twenty-one to James Fulton." She looked up at Winston. "Your father, of course. I've quite a bit about her in here. He is in another volume."

"You have your own sister in one of your books?" Winston blurted in surprise. He couldn't help himself. He'd known Aunt Rosemary liked to keep tabs on everyone, but...even her own sister?

Aunt Rosemary raised a brow. "You have an objection to my method of keeping records?"

"Not at all," Millie said. "In fact, we are incredibly grateful. I think that's what Winston meant."

Winston squeezed her hand. Millie always knew just what to say. "Yes, indeed. We are so grateful for you, Aunt Rosemary."

She sniffed. "As you should be. Now, let's see...is there anything useful in here?" She flipped through the pages, frowning now and again.

"I'm sure you have a good deal in there," Winston said, after they'd watched her for a moment. "Likely, we don't need to know it all. But is there anything you think might be useful?"

"Or even something you've not written down?" Millie asked.

"My dear, I write it all down," Aunt Rosemary said. "The memory fades, but the ink...never. I only buy the best."

His aunt was quiet for a long moment as she read a page. Finally, she asked, "Were you ever able to get a good look at the man you saw watching the house?"

He and Millie shook their heads. Aunt Rosemary went back to her book, tapping one long, wrinkled finger on the page. There was a thoughtful look on her face.

"You know something," Winston said. It wasn't worded as a question, but a fact. He could see it on her face.

"Perhaps," his aunt replied. She closed the book, set it down, and took a long sip of her tea. "But give me time to look further into this."

Winston nodded, and saw Millie doing the same.

"Now then," Aunt Rosemary said, "How is your father, dear?" She sipped her tea and raised her eyebrows in such a way she made it known the topic of his mother had ended.

As they finished their tea and made polite conversation, Winston couldn't help but be distracted. It was obvious his aunt knew more than she was telling him.

He only hoped that meant what she had to say wasn't something that was going to be upsetting when he found out.

Chapter 17

Millie wasn't quite sure what to think. When they'd left Winston's aunt's home, she felt as though she had more questions than ever. She glanced over at Winston as they walked along the street. "Do you think your aunt knows something?" she asked.

"Undoubtedly," Winston said. "Once she verifies whatever thought she'd had, I think we will hear from her."

"I wonder how long that will take," Millie said.

"I'm as anxious as you are," Winston said, squeezing her hand. "But knowing Aunt Rosemary, it won't be long at all. Let's take our minds off of it for a little. Didn't your father suggest a park?"

Millie smiled. "Yes."

"Then that is where we will go," Winston said, as he nodded in the direction.

They meandered through the streets and slowly drew near to the park. Colors exploded everywhere, as mid-summer growth seemed at its peak. Roses were everywhere it seemed, along with a dozen flowers Millie didn't know the names of, only that she loved their varying shades of purple, orange, and pink.

Neither of them spoke. Millie wondered if Winston was thinking about his mother's dilemma, like she was.

They walked for nearly an hour, stopping once to buy a drink, then slowly started back toward the house.

"I'll get a carriage if you like," Winston offered.

"No, I don't mind walking," Millie said, shaking her head. "It's such a wonderful day, and it's perfect for simply taking in the air. Papa was right."

"He's right about a good many things," Winston said. He smiled at her with such warmth it filled her. "Most of all, that you are perfect for me."

She rested her head on his shoulder for a moment. "As you are for me. I'll be forever indebted to my father and your aunt."

"Ah, don't tell her that," Winston warned. "She'll never forget that! Might even put it into one of her books."

Millie laughed. She could see that about the woman. It didn't make it less true though. She was grateful things had worked out as they had.

Not five minutes later, their street opened before them, and on it appeared to be a large crowd. "What's happening?" Millie asked, concern filling her at the unusual sight.

Winston frowned. "I don't know," he said.

They hastened their steps, and as they got closer, saw that the crowd seemed to be near their home. "Oh dear," Millie whispered.

Winson's long legs carried him swiftly, and Millie struggled to keep up. She scurried after him, then breathed a sigh of relief upon noticing that the crowd wasn't at their home, but was further past it.

"What's going on?" Winston questioned a neighbor as they came alongside him.

"Some fellow broke into the dentist's house," the man said, pointing to the police officers. "Lucky the officers were nearby on patrol."

"Lucky indeed," Winston said, as they watched.

The policemen had a man in their custody. A rough looking man with a pale face and cropped curly hair. As he was loaded into the police carriage, one of the officers caught sight of them and walked over.

"A moment of your time, Dr. Fulton?" he asked.

"Certainly," Winston said.

"We think this man might be the one who broke into your office," the policeman said. "The investigator is going to talk to him, and we'll send someone around this evening to update you. I just thought you and Mrs. Fulton might want to know."

"Thank you," Winston said.

Millie echoed him, then watched as the police drove away, and the crowd slowly dispersed. "It might be over," she said with a sigh. "All that worry of a criminal on the loose."

"I'll be waiting eagerly to hear from them this evening," Winston agreed.

They walked inside of the house. Winston went to his office, while Millie followed him.

The rest of the day passed by slowly. Dinner began and the police still hadn't stopped by. "Do you think they've forgotten?" Millie asked, feeling a little anxious as she stabbed at her boiled carrots.

"I hope not," Mother Nola said. She took a bite of roast pork. "I've had quite enough with worrying over the house being broken into. Winston, this wasn't what I expected when I moved here. I thought you lived in a quiet place."

"Ordinarily, that's true," Winston said. "I cannot believe that there have been two break-ins. Thankfully, with the man caught, and a higher police presence, that should be the last of that."

Millie's father nodded and buttered a roll. He'd been invited to stay for dinner. "I should think so," he agreed. "Nothing like being caught to deter any would-be criminals."

"I only hope—" Winston started, then was interrupted by a loud knock at the front door. "That might be the police," he said, getting up quickly.

He went to the door and a moment later returned with Investigator Jones. "Evening, everyone," the policeman said. "I just wanted to let you know that the man who broke into your office has been apprehended."

"How do you know that was him?" Millie asked.

"Easy enough," the investigator said. "In his coat pocket was an empty bottle of laudanum, and it had your name on it, Dr. Fulton. The bottle size was that of which you'd told me was missing."

"Then it's over," Mother Nola said, looking relieved. Then she sniffed. "Thank goodness. Took you long enough, but at least it's done."

"Yes, ma'am," Investigator Jones said with a tight smile. "Some things can't be rushed."

"We appreciate your efforts," Winston said, "and I am sure tonight we will each be sleeping more soundly."

Millie nodded. That part was true. Though she felt safe with Winston nearby, there had been a nervousness deep within her that she knew was attributed to the disruption and terrible violation of Winston's practice being broken into.

As the investigator left, and everyone returned to their meal, a terrible thought suddenly came to Millie.

She'd seen the man responsible for the damage and theft taken away. He looked nothing at all like the man who had been watching their home and talking with Mother Nola.

So, who was the man in the gray coat?

Chapter 18

"Just take two spoonfuls of this before bed and two again in the morning," Winston said, as he handed over the medicine to his patient. "Come see me or Dr. Husdon in three days if you are still feeling poorly."

Nodding, the patient left, and Winston returned to his examination room to quickly reset it for whoever he would be seeing next.

The last several days had been a delight. He had slept well, for starters. There was a feeling of peace knowing that the criminals were off of the street. His mother had also seemed in a good mood. To witness that alarmed him slightly, and truthfully, it made Millie nervous, but it was still a nice change from her picking at Millie or dropping endless remarks about who he should have married.

Millie entered the door between the office and house, holding a tray. "I've brought you something to drink," she told him. "You've a short break before your next patient."

"Wonderful," Winston said, and took one of the cups. Millie was incredibly thoughtful, and he would never not feel grateful. "Is all well in the house?"

"It appears to be," Millie said. "I wasn't there but for a few moments, however, your mother didn't stop me to ask for anything or to complain about me." She giggled. "That's an improvement, I suppose."

"I'm sorry," Winston said, regret on his face, he was sure. He felt it over every inch of his body and deeply inside. He had no idea when he married the terrible emotional toll it would take on Millie, as she suffered through his mother's callousness.

"Don't be," Millie answered with that smile of hers he loved. "While I didn't know what to expect when your mother moved in with us, I wouldn't trade it for anything because it means I have you."

As his heart swelled, Winston pulled Millie in for a hug. He would have kissed her too, but the office door opened just then and a mother and her child entered.

It was back to work.

The rest of the day passed by quickly, and before Winston knew it, he was dropping his notepad on Millie's desk.

"I'll copy these over for you," she said, picking up her pen.

"It can wait until tomorrow, if you like," Winston told her.

"Very well," Millie agreed. "I'll head in to the house."

"I'll join you right after I lock the door," Winston said.

He made sure the door was secured, and each window as well. After the recent events, he'd been much more careful with that.

As he walked inside the house, he tensed. Whatever good mood his mother had been in during the recent days had obviously ended. She seemed distressed, and was rummaging around in the parlor.

"Mother Nola, if you'll just tell me what you are looking for," Millie offered, "then I can help you."

"If I wanted your help, I'd have asked for it," his mother snapped.

"Mother," Winston said, stepping into the room. "That was uncalled for. Millie was offering to assist. There's no need to bark at her. Whatever is the matter?"

"Nothing. I've mislaid something, that's all." His mother picked up the cushions on the small sofa and replaced them.

"Perhaps we can help you look for it," Winston said. He kept his voice calm, sensing her obvious upset.

"I don't want help," she answered, and walked toward the kitchen, muttering.

He caught Millie's eyes. She shrugged. "I don't know."

Winston sighed. His mother could be like this at times, but usually she would say what had agitated her. Losing something would, of course. That was a bothersome and upsetting thing for anyone, but why wouldn't she say what it was she'd lost?

There was simply no reason to be this way. Unless...

"Millie," Winston said, his voice low, "I think she doesn't want us to know what is missing. Because something is wrong."

"It would appear that way," Millie agreed with a sigh. "I just wish she'd trust us. Let us help in some way. Oh, I do hope your aunt finds out something soon."

"I'll write her tonight," Winston said.

"That's a good idea," she said. "I'm going to go check on dinner."

"I'll be along after I've changed my clothes," Winston said.

He'd just started toward the stairs when there was a quiet knock at the front door. He turned and opened it, looking at the young boy before him. "Hello, how can I help you?"

"I've a note for Mrs. Fulton," the boy answered.

"I'll give it to her," Winston assured him, and reached out his hand.

The boy didn't hand it to him. "I don't know. The man told me not to give it to anyone but her."

"Oh? What man?" Winston asked. He reached into his pocket where he had several coins.

"I dunno." The boy hesitated. "He paid me pretty good though."

"What did he look like?" Winston asked.

"I dunno. Didn't seem much of him. Gray coat, a hat." The boy shrugged. "But I guess you can have it."

Winston handed the boy the coins and took the note. "Thank you. I promise to give it right to her."

The boy nodded, then ran off as quickly as he had come.

After he shut the door, Winston glanced down at the scrap of paper. It was an advertisement for shaving soap. "Hmm. Best shave?" he mused. "Clean scent and good for the skin? Why would this be so important to give to Millie?"

As he turned hastily, the paper rustled in the movement. His eye caught the handwriting on the backside of the advertisement.

Meet me at the usual spot.

Winston stilled. Just then, his mother came down the stairs hurrying toward him. She was wearing her favorite hat and holding her handbag.

"That's mine," she said, snatching the paper from him. She hurried past, opening and closing the front door behind her before he'd hardly blinked.

Winston stared at his hand a moment where the paper had been, and then the doorway his mother had just gone through. Then it hit him. Neither the advertisement nor the scrawl on the backside had been meant for Millie. The intended recipient was his mother! Then the boy's words struck him. The paper had come from a man in a gray coat.

"Millie!" Winston called, moving quickly toward the kitchen. "Millie!"

"What's the matter?" Millie gasped, rushing toward him.

"My mother. A note. The boy was...she's gone!" he blurted out, all of his words blending together.

"I can't understand you," Millie said. "Try again."

Winston closed his eyes and breathed in deeply. What was the matter with him? As a doctor, he was used to working under pressure. How was it he was stammering so? When he opened his eyes, he tried again.

"A boy came to the door with a note. I thought it was for you, as he said for Mrs. Fulton."

"Oh. Where is it? Was it from Papa?" Millie asked.

"No, Mother took it, and said it was for her." Winston ran a hand over his jaw. "That's not it though."

"Then what is it?" Millie asked.

Winston sensed the impatience in her voice. Rightfully so. The longer it took him to explain, the more time passed to prevent something untoward from happening with his mother.

He cleared his throat. "The note said, '*Meet me at the usual spot*.'"

"The usual spot?" Millie frowned. "And you say your mother took it?"

"Snatched it, is more like it," Winston said. "Where do you think the usual spot is? And should we send for the police?"

"I don't know if your mother would appreciate us contacting the police," Millie said. She dashed off and returned a moment later with her hat and handbag. "But I suspect I do know where the usual place is."

She opened the door and Winston gaped at her. "Where are you going?"

Millie turned with a surprised look. "To follow your mother, of course. Aren't you coming?"

Winston blinked several times, then nodded. "Right. Yes. I am." He hurried after Millie as they rushed down the sidewalk.

He only hoped they weren't too late to save his mother from whatever was happening—even if it were just herself.

Chapter 19

Like before, Millie stayed a short distance behind Mother Nola and the strange man. Not so far that she'd lose them, but not so close that she'd be spotted.

At least, she hoped. This whole following someone thing wasn't something she was the least bit experienced in, but she was certainly doing her best to blend in and be inconspicuous.

The same could not be said for Winston, though she suspected that wasn't through any fault of his. He kept up with her, but he also wore a panicked look on his face, as frequently someone would pass by and say, "Doctor," in greeting.

They both hoped his mother wouldn't overhear.

Mother Nola moved with a determined speed and soon reached the park. Their meeting spot must have been that one particular bench, for not long after entering the park, Millie found herself watching from the same area she had last time she'd followed Winston's mother here.

"I can't hear them," Winston whispered. "What's he saying?"

Mother Nola and the man with the gray jacket were sitting on a bench. However, their backs were to them, so Millie couldn't answer. She had no idea what they were discussing.

"Let's move closer," Winston suggested, and took a step forward.

"Wait," Millie said, and tugged on his sleeve.

Mother Nola and the man stood, and slowly walked over to a fountain in the park. Millie squinted, analyzing the older woman's face. She didn't seem concerned, fearful, or distressed. In fact, if anything, she seemed to be enjoying herself.

Millie and Winston followed behind, a dozen paces away. Millie was worried about being so close, but Mother Nola didn't seem to notice her whatsoever. She was able to see her mother-in-law's face better when she and the man paused at a young girl selling small bouquets of flowers.

After looking carefully at each, Mother Nola chose one. The man paid the girl, and Mother Nola held it as they walked, smiling up at the man.

Why in the world had he bought her flowers? The only explanation for that, and the smiles, and perhaps even the secrecy was that they were...

Millie turned to Winston. His eyes were as wide as hers. "Do you think," Millie started, then shook her head. It was a foolish idea. She couldn't finish it.

However, it was obvious Winston was thinking the same as her.

"I don't know," he answered, his voice hushed. "But it certainly seems that Mother isn't being blackmailed or threatened in any way. In fact, it seems she's..." He stared at her, seemingly lost for words.

She decided to speak what had come to mind. "In love?" Millie asked with a smile.

"Yes," Winston whispered.

Millie laughed and grabbed his arm. "Then perhaps we should leave them to enjoy the rest of their outing and return home."

"Perhaps," Winston said, though he looked slightly unsure.

Neither of them spoke on the walk back. Millie imagined Winston was just as lost in his thoughts as she was. After all, the idea of Mother Nola in love and sneaking about like a young girl was more than a little shocking.

As they came to the house, Winston paused to look at a carriage pulling alongside their house. Aunt Rosemary climbed out, then walked toward the front door.

"Aunt Rosemary," Winston called out, as he and Millie hurried closer.

"Winston! My dear boy," his aunt said. Then she turned to Millie, "Good to see you, Millie dear. I've got...news." She raised her eyebrows in a dramatic way.

"So do we," Millie answered with a grin. "You'll never guess what we just saw."

"Tell me," Winston's aunt demanded as they walked into the parlor.

"Should I get tea?" Millie asked. "Let me do that. Winston can tell you what we just observed."

She hurried away into the kitchen, returning a short time later with tea and cookies. As she set the tray down, Millie was surprised to see Aunt Rosemary didn't look the least bit shocked. Had Winston not told her their revelation about his mother?

Taking her tea, Aunt Rosemary started to talk. "Two years before your mother married your father," she began without preamble, "your mother fell in love with a young man. Her parents didn't agree, as he was of a much lower social standing and wouldn't have been able to provide for her. Her heart was broken, and she swore to me she'd never love again."

Millie glanced at Winston as she offered him a cup and sat next to him on the small sofa. He didn't say anything, but his face held an expression of surprise.

"I didn't know this," Winston said.

"That's not unexpected. When she met your father, it was not love at first sight for her, or even second. However, after a year of persistently pursing the woman he knew he wanted to spend the rest of his life with, your father was rewarded when your mother agreed." Aunt Rosemary took a slow sip of her tea.

"This is a fascinating story," Winston said, "but I'm afraid I don't understand where the man in the gray or mother's sneaking about comes into play. If she's simply in love again, then why wouldn't she just say so?"

His aunt shook her head. "It's not simply that she's in love, dear boy. It's *who* she's in love with. My sources say it is the man she'd been in love with before she married your father. Evidently, their paths have crossed and they are pursuing the love that they once shared. He's still a writer. A...*novelist*." Aunt Rosemary shuddered and put a hand to her heart. "Can you imagine? What is she thinking? A creator of fictitious tales!"

Millie snorted, and when Winston stared at her, couldn't stop the giggles that burst out. Once she got hold of herself, she said, "I apologize. But, don't you see what's happened?"

At his headshake, she continued, "The older gray jacket. Them slipping out, trading letters, not wanting to be seen. It must mean that he's of a lower class still, at least financially, even if he's possibly made a success with his writing. All this must be because your mother doesn't want anyone to know or to cause a scandal. It's obvious she is fearful of her reputation."

"Or yours," Aunt Rosemary said, gesturing with a sugar cookie. "She might be of the age she doesn't care any longer, but is concerned about your reputation as a doctor, Winston." She fixed him with a stern look. "I should think you would be concerned too. Should a man such as that be part of your family?"

"That's a foolish question," Winston said. "Times are changing, Aunt Rosemary. Concern over the classes as well. Look at Rose and Levi—"

"Do not remind me," his aunt said in her throaty voice, closing her eyes and giving a pained expression.

Winston continued. "I just want Mother to be content. As long as this man isn't one who would take advantage of her, then I'm happy for her. You should be as well. After all, she is family."

"I'm even happier," Millie said, "for if this is true, then she will have to stop complaining I am of a low class and you took pity on me." She paused. "It does get tiresome to hear that so frequently," she confessed.

Millie realized that Mother Nola, who felt so proud and almost obsessed with her ideas of social class, might actually be holding herself back from something she'd been longing for most of her life—true love. Love wasn't something that a person could control. Mother Nola's refusal to admit that was leading to incredible loneliness, and Millie felt sad for her.

Winston took her hand and kissed it. "I think it is the other way around. It is you who took pity upon me," he said, "and the fact that you knew I'd waste away without you."

"But what are you going to do?" Aunt Rosemary asked. Concern was etched into every one of her wrinkles. "The longer she continues to sulk around like a criminal, the more obvious it will become. While you might be willing to accept this man into your family, her actions are simply making the situation look..." she waved her hand around, "as though she's lost her mind or intent on the destruction of her reputation."

Millie glanced at Winston. "She's right. Your mother's reputation is very important to her, and others will start to talk. That isn't something she will want, but it's possible she has no idea it is happening or will happen. But your mother also gets so defensive whenever we approach her. How can we help her?"

Winston sighed deeply, and focused his attention outside the window.

It was a beautiful day. The sky was a bright blue and the few clouds were wispy, light and airy. It was such a contrast to how he felt right now, heavy with the burden of indecision. It seemed almost unfair. While others walked carefree past the parlor window, he was here worrying over his mother.

Millie touched his hand gently and brought him back to the present moment. "I really have no idea," he admitted. "We must think of something, though."

"Yes, someone must," Aunt Rosemary agreed. She stood then. "I'll be going. If you'd like me to talk with her, tell her she's making an obvious fool of herself, and at her age, I'd be happy to. She is my sister, after all. But not today. This afternoon, I'm having a young woman over for tea."

"Is there a young man who will just so happen to stop by and call?" Winston asked with a chuckle.

"Perhaps," his aunt smiled. "I must do what I do best." She embraced Millie and kissed her cheek. "And that is putting together successful matches. Like you. And Levi and Rose." She pinched Winston's cheek. "Now, I must be on my way. Let me know if you need my help."

She left quickly, seeing herself out, and Millie studied the carriage through the window as it left. "I don't know. It is generous your aunt has offered to talk to your mother for us, but that doesn't seem the right way to do this," she said. "She's in love. This is a second chance at something she wasn't able to have before. She's not making a fool of herself."

"Yet," Winston corrected her. "If she doesn't tell us, and continues to go about hiding her relationship, she will be ousted at some point, and not by a friendly face. That would be devastating to her. It's likely Mother has no idea that anyone knows she's been seen with him. No, we must let her know that we know, and face the consequences of whatever that might be."

As he stood, pacing in the small room, Millie couldn't help but feel relief that what was once her dilemma was now also Winston's. Confronting Mother Nola with the news they knew who this man was wouldn't make her happy at all.

Chapter 20

Winston tapped his fingers on his desk. He felt anxious. Never in his life had he ever questioned his mother the way he had recently. What was upsetting was the fact he'd need to do it again.

If she simply continued on the way she was, it was only a matter of time before one of her friends saw her with this man, whatever his name might be. The fact that he was of a lower class was of no consequence to him, however it was apparent it was to his mother because of how clandestine she was being in her behavior.

How could he convince her that there was no reason to hide? Nothing to be ashamed of. That was where he was stuck, and he desperately wanted to figure out his words before he approached her. And possibly made a mess of the situation.

"Mother," he practiced, "class means nothing. Look at my marriage with Millie."

No, that wouldn't do. It could also quite possibly hurt Millie's feelings. He'd best try again.

"Mother, you've upset Aunt Rosemary. She says people are talking..."

No, that wasn't right either. He huffed out a sigh and looked upward. How? How was he to word his concerns?

Winston rose and entered the house. His nerves were rattled. A warm drink would soothe them.

He poured from the kettle and tried again. "Mother, I know you've been sneaking out to see a man. There's no use denying it. Millie and I followed you."

There was a gasp, and Winston turned, nearly splashing his tea everywhere. His mother stood in the doorway, one hand to her throat. "Winston!" she said, with a mixture of shock and anger. "You've been following me?"

Winston swallowed hard and set down his tea. This wasn't how he'd envisioned the conversation. But there he was. "Yes, Mother. I have."

"Because you don't trust me?" she asked, her eyes narrowing.

"No, because I love you and I was worried," Winston said, stepping closer. "You've been rather secretive as of late, and I was concerned."

"Concerned? More like nosey," his mother sniffed. "If you've forgotten, Winston, I am a grown woman who is more than capable of taking care of herself."

"But evidently not capable of keeping your relationship secretive," Winston said wryly. "Aunt Rosemary has heard whisperings, and asked me what you were up to."

"Rosemary?" His mother paled then and sank into one of the wooden chairs in front of the small kitchen table. She didn't speak, and Winston wondered if he should get his doctor's bag. She didn't look well.

"Are you alright?" Winston finally asked.

His mother looked up at him then, her face red with anger. Her voice got higher with each word. "What do you think? You've intruded in my personal business. You've treated me with no respect. That isn't how I raised you to be!"

Millie walked into the kitchen. She looked as though she wanted to walk back out, but instead, she sat at the table. Winston felt an immense gratitude for her being there right now. It was as he feared, he'd messed up terribly.

"Mother Nola," Millie said softly, "you are right. That's not how you raised him to be."

Winston didn't miss his mother's smug look before it faded into confusion as Millie continued.

"You raised your son to be caring and concerned, full of love for the woman who took care of him and gave him everything he needed to become a successful man. You raised him to be conscientious of what others might need."

"It's true. I have," his mother answered, straightening her shoulders. Her voice still wobbled slightly, but her eyes were fixed on Millie.

"It is only natural then," Millie went on, "that the same instincts are engaged when he is concerned about your wellbeing. We know it can not be easy being a widow. We also know that you had fallen in love once, many years before you met Winston's father, and that you might have a chance to rekindle that friendship or have it turn into more."

His mother stiffened, but didn't speak, as Millie reached over and rested her hand on top of his mother's.

"We are overjoyed for you. We want you to be able to be open about this friendship, and whatever it turns into, not hide it as though you are ashamed. There is no reason to be that way. This man, whoever he is, surely must hold a special place in your heart, and we'd like to extend the same."

Winston's mother swallowed visibly. "Is...is that so?" she asked quietly.

"It is," Millie smiled. "We know there's room in your heart for your first husband, Winston, and anyone else who comes along. Winston and I worry and question from a place of love. We want what's best for you, just like how you want what's best for Winston."

"It's true, Mother," Winston said, dropping in the chair next to her. "Only, Millie is much better at saying it than I am."

"Your strengths lie in other areas," his mother said, taking one of her hands and squeezing his. He saw she hadn't moved hers from Millie's grasp.

With a sigh, she said, "Millie, I apologize. You have been nothing but kind to this fussy woman, welcoming me into your home and life and assuring me of your devotion. I suppose I was not wanting to become accepting of your lower station as it meant a friendship—or more—with my old acquaintance might mean I was also lowering myself and my standards I was raised upon."

"None of that matters to us," Millie said. "Times are changing. If you truly love this man, then does it matter if you have more money than he does? Or is it more important to make up for lost time?"

His mother nodded, and a calm look came over her face. She squeezed their hands before pulling away. "You are right. Charles and I lost too much time. Not everyone gets a second chance for something. I would be a fool not to make the most of this."

Winston nodded and smiled at her, then at Millie, taking her hand.

"You ought to know," his mother continued, taking a deep breath. "He has asked me to marry him. I am seriously considering it."

Millie gasped and hugged his mother. She froze for a moment, then returned the embrace.

"Well then," Winston said. "When do we get to meet him properly like? None of that lurking about and hiding across the street."

His mother smiled. "Tomorrow," she promised. "I'll tell him now."

She exited the room, and Winston turned to Millie. "You have wonderful timing," he told her. "I was about to make a terrible mess. I'd started spectacularly, actually. Things were getting bad quickly. And you...you smoothed everything over. Said it all perfectly."

"I have a way of doing that," Millie agreed, then laughed. "I meant what I said though. I think it's wonderful. Your mother deserves happiness."

"So do we," Winston said. He leaned back in the chair and sighed. "Now comes the hard part of all of this."

Millie stared at him. "There's something harder than what we've been through?" she asked, incredulously.

"Yes," Winston said. He stood and held his hand out to her. "Will you go with me to Aunt Rosemary and convince her that this is a good idea? I think we will need your way with words."

Millie laughed, and Winston knew he'd never tire of that sound or her smile or anything else about her.

But he had been quite serious. Aunt Rosemary could be a little scary. Luckily, he had Millie. With her by his side, he was confident everything would turn out fine.

After he finished with his patients that afternoon, Millie's father kindly seeing to the final two, he and Millie knocked on Aunt Rosemary's door to attempt to explain what had happened. She opened it, her arms stretched out in welcome. "You are just in time," she said throatily, stepping back. "Come in, both of you."

"In time for what?" Millie asked.

"For tea, and to meet this couple that I've just put together. It was another successful match," Aunt Rosemary proclaimed, then set off at a brisk pace.

Winston and Millie hurried behind her. "Won't we be intruding?" Millie asked.

"Not at all. We're family, are we not?" Aunt Rosemary said, and opened the parlor door. "You already know Nola. Meet Charles Harpin. A fine writer, if ever there was. A novelist of the highest caliber."

Winston felt as though his eyes were about to burst from the sockets. That was not the way she'd referred to him earlier. "Aunt Rosemary—"

She turned and faced him with such a glare he took a step back. Once again, Millie came to his rescue.

"My goodness," she gasped. "Aren't you the perfect matchmaker. I know how much Mother Nola loves to read! Oh, Aunt Rosemary! You are wonderful at what you do."

Aunt Rosemary gave his wife an approving smile, sniffed at him, and then walked into the parlor.

Winston followed. "Remind me never to never mention that *we* had anything to do with this," he whispered to Millie. "Somehow, I have the feeling Aunt Rosemary won't like that."

She simply winked at him, then hurried forward to meet her future... father-in-law?

Epilogue

"Do you have everything?" Millie called down from the top of the stairs.

"Yes! Oh! No! I think I left my hat up there," Mother Nola said, as she felt the top of her head.

"I'll look," Millie said, and hurried into Mother Nola's bedroom. She found the hat on the bed, along with one of Charles's novels, and hurried down the stairs. "You almost forgot this book," she said.

"Thankfully, we won't be living far away. If there's anything else, I can get it easily," Mother Nola said, putting her hat on and adjusting it in the foyer mirror.

"I can hardly believe you are about to be married," Millie said. She checked the time. "We must hurry, so you aren't late."

Her mother-in-law turned around and faced her then. "Millie, if it doesn't work out, can I come back here?"

Millie blinked. She hadn't expected that question. Not after all that had happened. "Of course, you can. But why wouldn't things work out?"

"Well, you see, I've not met Charle's mother. What if…"

"Don't worry," Millie said kindly. "I'm sure your mother-in-law will treat you just the same way you treat me."

Mother Nola sank into a chair, horror on her face. "Then I'm doomed," she said, burying her face into her hands.

Suppressing her smile, Millie shook her head and gently placed her hand on the older woman's shoulder. "The way you *treat* me," she clarified. "Not the way you *treated* me."

Dropping her hands, Mother Nola brightened. "Do you…think so?"

"While I don't know so, I will hope so," Millie answered.

There was a knock on the door and she hurried to get it. Before her was Mr. Harpin, with a much older woman she could only assume was his mother, and Mother Nola's new mother-in-law.

The woman, tall, thin, and with sharp eyes, looked past Millie to Mother Nola. With a loud sniff, she said, "So. You must be my new daughter-in-law. I hear you are rich. Good. My son works hard for what he has and doesn't need it frittered away."

Mother Nola grabbed hold of Millie's arm and glanced at her with worry in her eyes. Millie smiled reassuringly at her, and then turned to Mrs. Harpin. "Hello, I'm Millie. We're delighted to meet you."

Past their shoulders, she could see Winston starting up the walkway. He was laughing, and Millie felt it bubble up inside of her too.

"Let me get your bags, Mother," Winston said, as he approached. "We will miss you. But all of you are welcome, at any point. We'll see you momentarily at the judge's chambers. Millie's father is attending patients for me."

"I'll help you," Mr. Harpin said, grabbing one of the bags.

"Hurry now," Mrs. Harpin snapped over her shoulder as she walked to the carriage. "Don't keep us waiting. My Charles is too important of a man to be held up."

They all left, Mother Nola with a last panicked look over her shoulder. "She'll be fine," Winston said, as he closed the door, and once the carriage drove away, he burst out laughing.

"Oh, poor Mother Nola," Millie said. She brought her hands to her face, then dropped them to twist her fingers together. "I'm not sure she can handle that. We'd best hurry to catch up with them."

"She won't have to," he chuckled, wiping at his eyes. "Mr. Harpin said his mother was doing that to scare her a bit, because she heard how rough of a time you'd had at first. Really, she's a sweet lady."

"Oh, that's a relief!" Millie said. She leaned into Winston.

He wrapped his arms around her. "And now, it's just us."

"For a few months, anyway," Millie agreed. She headed toward the kitchen. "Would you like a snack before we leave? I'm famished."

"Yes, that sounds—wait! What do you mean a few months? Is someone else moving in? Millie? Millie!"

Millie giggled to herself as she cut a large slice of pound cake and Winston came rushing into the room. As he gaped at her, she simply smiled and nodded, patting her stomach. "Here you are," she said, sliding him a slice of cake and taking the larger for herself. "*I* am eating for two now."

Keep reading

Did you enjoy meeting Aunt Rosemary? She's *quite* a character. See much more of her in Rose and Levi's story, *Romancing the Wrangler*. Also, follow me to see her next appearance, coming early 2025!

***

Rose and Levi only have one rule—make their own rules.

Free spirited Rose Alden is her father's youngest child, and his disappointment. Her sharp mind and wit are matched only by her sarcastic tongue and disobedience in finding a suitable husband like her older sisters did. She's desperate to live her own life, make her own rules, and marriage is not something she is interested in.

Ranch hand Levi Patterson understands just how Rose feels. It's why he's grateful to be working for her father on the Alden's quiet ranch. However, the past he thought he'd left behind has caught up, demanding he choose between the needs of others and his own.

A sudden change of events forces them each to make a decision that will change the future forever. Will Rose fight for what she longs for? Can Levi return to what was, or will he continue to blaze his own path with Rose by his side?

Find it on Amazon: https://www.amazon.com/Romancing-Wrangler-Second -Chance-Groom-ebook/dp/B0CFWJB2W4

Want a free book?

Thank you for taking the time to read Millie's Wedding Dilemma!

Could I ask for one small favor? Reviews like yours on Amazon mean so much to me and help others to find my books! Even just a single line means a lot!

Also...

Want a FREE book?

Stop by my website to get your no strings attached **FREE book**. It's my gift to you, as a thank you for reading this one.

www.sarahlambbooks.com

About the Author

Sarah is wife to an amazing teacher and mom to two boys who are growing up just a little too fast. She spends her days working and writing in the Blue Ridge Mountains.

There are other great books in this series as well!

Find all the Matchmaker and Mother-in-lawbooks on Amazon!

https://www.amazon.com/dp/B0CS4S1W CP

***

Want more of Sarah's books? She writes for children and adults! Find them all on Amazon!

https://www.amazon.com/stores/Sarah-Lamb/author/B098H3SGLK